This book
belongs to HOPE

THE PURITAN TWINS

By Lucy Fitch Perkins

ILLUSTRATED BY THE AUTHOR

BOSTON AND NEW YORK
HOUGHTON MIFFLIN COMPANY
The Riverside Press Cambridge
1921

R0127300820

JFIC P41 pu

CONTENTS

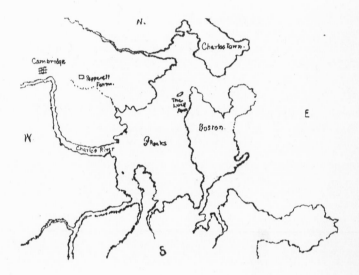

I
THE PEPPERELLS AND THE CAPTAIN

I

THE PEPPERELLS AND THE CAPTAIN

ONE bright warm noonday in May of the year 1638, Goodwife Pepperell opened the door of her little log cabin, and, screening her eyes from the sun with a toilworn hand, looked about in every direction as if searching for some one. She was a tall, spare woman, with a firm mouth, keen blue eyes, and a look of patient endurance in her face, bred by the stern life of pioneer New England. Far away across the pasture which sloped southward from the cabin she could see long meadow grass waving in the breeze, and beyond a thread of blue water where the Charles River flowed lazily to the sea. Westward there was also pasture land where sheep were grazing, and in the distance a glimpse of the thatched roofs of the little village of Cambridge.

Goodwife Pepperell gazed long and earnestly in this direction, and then, making a trumpet of her hands, sent a call ringing across the silent fields. "Nancy! Daniel!" she shouted.

She was answered only by the tinkle of sheep bells. A shade of anxiety clouded the blue eyes as she went round to the back of the cabin and looked toward the dense forest which bounded her vision on the north. Stout-hearted though she was, Goodwife Pepperell could never forget the terrors which lay concealed behind that mysterious rampart of green. Not only were there wolves and deer and many other wild creatures hidden in its depths, but it sheltered also the perpetual menace of the Indians. Toward the east, at some distance from the cabin, corn-fields stretched to salt meadows, and beyond, across the bay, she could see the three hills of Boston town.[1]

[1] See map.

As no answering shout greeted her from this direction either, the Goodwife stepped quickly toward a hollow stump which stood a short distance from the cabin. Beside the stump a slender birch tree bent beneath the weight of a large circular piece of wood hung to its top by a leather thong. This was the samp-mill, where their corn was pounded into meal. Seizing the birch tree with her hands, she brought the wooden pestle down into the hollow stump with a resounding thump. The birch tree sprang back lifting the block with it and again she pulled it down and struck the stump another blow, then paused to listen. This time there was, beside the echo, an answering shout, and in a few moments two heads appeared above the rows of young corn just peeping out of the ground, two pairs of lively bare feet came flying across the garden patch, and a breathless boy and girl stood beside their mother.

They were a sturdy pair of twelve-year-olds, the boy an inch or more taller than his sister, and both with the blue eyes, fair skin, and rosy cheeks which proclaimed their English blood. There was a gleam of pride in Goodwife Pepperell's eye as she looked at her children, but not for the world would she have let them see it; much less would she have owned it to herself, for she was a Puritan mother, and regarded pride of any kind as altogether sinful. "Where have you been all the morning?" she said. "You were nowhere to be seen and the corn is not yet high enough to hide you."

"I was hoeing beyond that clump of bushes," said Daniel, pointing to a group of high blueberries that had been allowed to remain in the cleared field.

"And I was keeping away the crows," said Nancy, holding out her wooden clappers. "Only I fell asleep. It was so warm I just couldn't help it."

"So shall thy poverty come as one that travelleth and thy want as an armed man," quoted the mother sternly. "Night is the time for sleep. Go now and eat the porridge

I have set for you in your little porringers, and then go down to the bay with this basket and fill it with clams. Put a layer of seaweed in the basket first and pack the clams in that. They will keep alive for some time if you bed them so, and be sure to bring back the shovel."

This was a task that suited the Twins much better than either hoeing corn or scaring crows, and they ran into the house at once, ate their porridge with more haste than good manners, and dashed joyfully away across the fields toward the river-mouth, a mile away. They followed a path across the wide stretch of pasture, where wild blackberry vines and tall blueberry bushes grew, then through a strip of meadow land, and at last ran out on the bare stretch of sand and weed left by the ebb tide toward the narrow channel cut by the clear water of the Charles.

Here they set down the basket and began looking about for the little holes which betray the hiding-places of clams.

7

"Oh, look, Dan," cried Nancy, stopping to admire the long line of foot-prints which they had left behind them. "Dost see what a pretty border we have made? 'T is just like a pattern." She walked along the edge of the stream with her toes turned well out, leaving a track in the sand like this: Then the delightful flat surface tempted her to further exploits. She

8

picked up a splinter of driftwood and, making a wide flourish, began to draw a picture. "See," she called rapturously to Dan, "this is going to be a pig! Here's his nose, and here's his curly tail, and here are his little fat legs." She clapped her hands with admiration. "Now I shall do something else," she announced as she finished the pig with a round red pebble stuck in for the eye. "Let me see. What shall I draw? Oh, I know! A picture of Gran'ther Wattles! Look, Dan."
She made a careful stroke. "Here's his nose, and here's his chin. They are monstrous near together 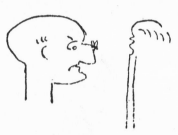 because he has nothing but gums between! And here's his long tithing-stick with the squirrel-tail on the end!"

"It doth bear a likeness to him!" admitted Dan, laughing in spite of himself, "but, sister, thou shouldst not mock him. He is an old man, and we should pay respect to gray hairs. Father says so."

"Truly I have as much of respect as he hath of hair," answered naughty Nancy. "His poll is nearly as bald as an egg."

"I know the cause of thy displeasure," declared Dan. "Gran'ther Wattles poked thee for bouncing about during the sermon last Sunday. But it is unseemly to bounce in the meeting-house, and besides, is he not the tithing-man? 'T is his duty to see that people behave as they should."

"He would mayhap have bounced himself if a bee had been buzzing about his nose as it did about mine," said Nancy, and, giving a vicious dab at the pictured features, she drew a bee perched on the end of Gran'ther Wattles's nose. "Here now are all the gray hairs he hath," she added, making three little scratches above the ear.

"Nancy Pepperell!" cried her brother, aghast, "dost thou not remember what happened to the forty and two children that said 'Go up, thou bald head' to Elijah? It

would be no marvel if bears were to come
out of the woods this moment to eat thee
up!"

"'T was n't Elijah, 't was Elisha," Nancy
retorted with spirit, "but it matters little
whether 't was one or t' other, for I don't
believe two bears could possibly hold so
much, and besides dost thou not think it a

deal worse to cause a bear to eat up forty and two children than to say 'Go up, thou bald head'?"

"Nancy!" exclaimed her horrified brother, glancing fearfully toward the forest and clapping his hand on her mouth to prevent further impiety, "thou art a wicked, wicked girl! Dost thou not know that the eye of the Lord is in every place? Without doubt his ear is too, and He can hear every word thy saucy tongue sayeth. Come, let us rub out this naughty picture quickly, and mayhap God will take no notice this time." He ran across Gran'ther Wattles's portrait from brow to chin, covering it with foot-prints. "Besides," he went on as he trotted back and forth, "thou hast broken a command-ment! Thou hast made a likeness of some-thing that's in the earth, and that's Gran'-ther Wattles! Nancy, thou dost take fearful chances with thy soul."

Nancy began to look a little anxious as she considered her conduct. "At any rate," she said defensively, "it isn't a graven im-

age, and I have neither bowed down to it
nor served it! I do try to be good, Dan,
but it seemeth that the devil is ever at my
elbow."

"'T is because thou art idle," said Dan,
shaking his head as gravely as Gran'ther
Wattles himself. "Busy thyself with the
clams, and Satan will have less chance

at thy idle hands, and thy idle tongue too."

Nancy obediently took hold of the basket which Dan thrust into her hands, and together they walked for some distance over the sandy stretches. Suddenly a tiny stream of water spouted up beside Dan's feet. "Here they be!" he shouted, plunging his shovel into the sand, "and what big ones!" Nancy surveyed the clams with disfavor. They were thrusting pale thick muscles out between the lobes of their shells. "They look as if they were sticking out their tongues at us," said Nancy as she picked one up gingerly and dropped it into the basket. "But, Dan, Mother said we were to bed them in seaweed!"

"I see none here," said Dan, leaning on his shovel and looking about him. "The tide hath swept everything as clean as a floor."

"I'll seek for some while thou art busy with the digging," said Nancy, glad to escape the duty of picking up the clams,

14

and off she trotted without another word.
The flats, seamed and grooved with channels where pools of water still lingered,
sloped gently down to the lower level of
the bay, and farther out a range of rocks
lifted themselves above the sandy waste.

"I'll surely find seaweed on the rocks," thought Nancy to herself as she sped along, and in a few moments she had reached them, had tossed up the basket, and was climbing their rugged sides.

"There's a mort o' seaweed here," she said, nodding her head wisely as she picked up a long string of kelp; "I can fill my basket in no time at all." There was no need for haste, she thought, so she sat down beside a pool of water left in a hollow of the rocks, to explore its contents. The first thing she found was a group of tiny barnacles, and for a while she amused herself by washing salt water over them to see them open their tiny cups of shell. In the pool itself a beautiful lavender-colored jellyfish was floating about, and just beyond lay a star-fish clinging to a bunch of seaweed. She found other treasures scattered about by the largess of the tide — tiny spiral shells, stones of all colors, and a horseshoe crab, besides seaweed with pretty little pods which popped delightfully when

16

she squeezed them with her fingers. Then
she heard the cries of gulls overhead and
watched them as they wheeled and circled
between her and the sky. When they flew
out to sea she sat with her hands clasping
her knees and gazed across the bay at the

17

three hills of Boston town. She could see quite plainly the tall beacon standing like a ship's mast on top of Beacon Hill, and farther north she strained her eyes to pick out Governor Winthrop's dwelling from the cluster of houses which straggled up the slope of Copp's Hill and which made all there was of the city of Boston in that early day.

For some time she sat there hugging her knees and thinking long, long thoughts, and it was not until the sound of little waves lapping against the rocks roused her that she woke from her day dream and realized with terror that the tide had turned. The channels and lower levels of the bay were already brimming over, and the water was deep about the rocks on which she perched. At almost the same moment Dan had been surprised by a cold wave which washed over his bare feet, and, turning about, was dismayed to find a sheet of blue water covering the bay and to see Nancy standing on the topmost rock shouting "Dan! Dan!"

at the top of her lungs. For one astonished instant he looked at her, then, throwing down his shovel, he plunged unhesitatingly into the icy bath. And now Nancy, realizing that there was not a moment to lose if she hoped to reach the shore in safety, let herself slowly down off the rocks, leaving the basket behind her, and started toward her brother.

The water was already so deep in the channels that their progress toward each other was slow, but they ploughed bravely on, feeling the bottom carefully at each step lest they sink in some sand-pocket or hollow washed out by the tide. Some distance away toward Charlestown a fishing schooner rocked on the deeper water of the bay, and a fisherman in a small boat, attracted by the shouting, looked up, and, seeing the two struggling figures, instantly bent to his oars and started toward them. Though he rowed rapidly, it was some minutes before he could reach the children, who were now floundering about in water nearly up to their necks.

"Hold fast to my shoulder, Nancy," he heard Dan cry. "I can float, and I can swim a little. Keep thy nose above water and let thy feet go where they will." Nancy, spluttering and gurgling, was trying hard to follow Dan's directions, when the boat shot alongside, and a cheery voice cried, "Ahoy, there! Come aboard, you young porpoises!"

To the children it was like a voice straight from heaven. Dan immediately helped Nancy to get into the boat, and then she balanced it while he climbed aboard.

When they were safely bestowed among the lobster-pots with which the boat was laden, the man leaned on his oars and eyed them critically. "Short of sense, ain't ye?" he remarked genially. "Nigh about drownded that time or I'm no skipper! If ye ain't bent on destruction ye'd better get into dry clothes. Ye're as wet as a mess of drownded kittens. Tell me where you live and I'll take you home."

He flung a tarpaulin over the shivering figures and tucked it around them as he scolded. "'T is all my fault," sobbed poor Nancy. "Dan came in just to get me out."

"Very commendable of him, I'm sure," said the stranger, nodding approvingly at Dan, "and just what he'd ought to do, and doubtless you're worth saving at that, though a hen-headeder young miss I never see in all my days!"

"She went to find seaweed to bed the clams," explained Dan, coming to his sister's defense, "and the tide caught her. Thou art kind indeed to pick us up, sir."

"Oh," groaned remorseful Nancy, her teeth chattering, "it's all because I'm such a sinner! I made a likeness of Gran'ther

Wattles in the sand and said dreadful things about the prophet Elijah, or mayhap 't was Elisha, and Dan said a bear might come to eat me up just like the forty and two children, and instead of a bear we both were almost swallowed by the tide!"

"Well, now," said the stranger, comfortingly, "ye see instead of sending bears the Lord sent me along to fish ye out, just the same as He sent the whale to swallow Jonah when he was acting contrary! Looks like He meant to let ye off with a scare this time. Come now, my lass, there's salt water enough aboard and if ye cry into the boat, ye'll have to bail her out. Besides," he added whimsically, looking up at the sky, "there's another squall coming on, and two at a time is too many for any sailor. If I'm to cast you up on the shore same as the whale, ye'll have to tell me which way to go, and who ye are."

"Our father is Josiah Pepperell," answered Dan, "and our house is almost a mile back from shore near Cambridge."

"So you're Josiah Pepperell's children! To be sure, to be sure! Might have known it. Ye do favor him some," said the fisherman. "Well! well! The ways of the Lord are surely past finding out! Why, I knew your father way back in England. He came over here for religion and I came for fish. Not that I ain't a God-fearing man," he added hastily, noticing a look of horror on Nancy's face, "but I ain't so pious as some. I'm a seafaring man, Captain Sanders of the Lucy Ann, Marblehead. Ye can see her riding at anchor out there in the bay. I haven't set eyes on your father since he left Boston and settled in the back woods up yonder."

He sent the boat flying through the water with swift, sure strokes as he talked, and brought it ashore at the first landing-place they found. Here they drew it up on the bank and, taking out the lobster-pots, turned it upside down so the rain would not fill it. Two great green lobsters with goblin-like eyes were hidden away under

23

the pots, and when the boat was overturned they tumbled out and started at a
lively pace for the water.

"Hi, there!" shouted the Captain, seizing them by their tails, "where are your
manners? By jolly, I like to forgot ye!
Come along now and take supper with the
Pepperells. I invite ye! They're short of
clams and they'll be pleased to see ye, or
I miss my reckoning." There were pegs
stuck in the scissor-like claws, so the creatures were harmless, and, swinging along
with one kicking vigorously in each hand,
the Captain plunged into the long meadow
grass, the children following close at his
heels.

The clouds grew darker and darker;
there was a rumble of thunder, and streaks
of lightning tore great rents in the sky as
they hurried across the open meadow and
struck into the pasture land beyond.

"Head into the wind there and keep going," shouted the Captain as the children
struggled along, impeded by their wet

24

clothing. "It's from the north, and we're pointed straight into it."

Past bushes waving distractedly in the wind, under the boughs of young oak trees, over stones and through briars they sped, and at last they came in sight of the cabin just as the storm broke. Goodwife Pepperell was standing in the door gazing anxiously toward the river, when they dashed out of the bushes and, scudding past her, stood dripping on the hearth-stone. Her husband was just hanging his gun over the chimney-piece, and the noise of their entrance was drowned out by a clap of thunder; so when he turned about and saw the three drenched figures it was no wonder that for an instant he was too surprised to speak.

"Well, of all things!" he said at last, holding out his hand to Captain Sanders. "What in God's providence brings thee here, Thomas? Thou art welcome indeed. 'T is a long time since I have seen thee."

"God's providence ye may call it," answered the Captain, shaking the Goodman's hand as if he were pumping out the hold of a sinking ship, "and I'll not gainsay it. The truth is I overhauled these small craft floundering around in the tide-wash with water over their scuppers 'n' all but wrecked, so I took 'em in tow and brought 'em ashore!"

Their mother, meanwhile, had not waited for explanations. Seeing how chilled they were, she had hurried the children to the loft above the one room of the cabin and was already giving them a rub-down and getting out dry clean clothes while they told her their adventure.

"Thank God you are safe," she said, clasping them both in her arms, when the tale was told.

"Thank Captain Sanders as well, Mother," said Daniel. "Had it not been for him, I doubt if we could have reached the shore."

"Let this be a lesson to you, then," said the Goodwife, loosening her clasp and pick-

26

ing up the wet clothing. "You know well about the tide! Nancy, child, why art thou so wild and reckless? Thou art the cause of much anxiety."

At her mother's reproof, gentle though it was, poor Nancy flopped over on her stomach, and, burying her face in her hands, gave way to tears.

"It's all because I am so wicked," she moaned. "My sins are as scarlet! Oh, Mother, dost think God will cause the lightning to strike us dead to punish me?" She shuddered with fear as a flash shone through the chinks of the logs and for an instant lighted the dim loft.

Her mother put down the wet clothes and, lifting her little daughter tenderly in her arms, laid her on her bed. "God maketh the rain to fall on both the just and the unjust," she said soothingly. "Rest here while I go down and get supper."

She covered her warmly with a homespun blanket, and, accompanied by Dan, made her way down the ladder. She found

27

her husband putting fresh logs on the fire and stirring the coals to a blaze, while the Captain hung his coat on the corner of the mantel-shelf to dry. She went up to him and held out her hand. "Captain Sanders," she said, "but for thee this might be a desolate household indeed this night."

The Captain's red face turned a deeper shade, and he fidgeted with embarrassment, as he took her hand in his great red paw, then dropped it suddenly as if it were hot. "Oh, stow it, ma'am, stow it," he begged. "That is, I mean to say — why, by jolly, ma'am, a pirate could do no less when he see a fine bit of cargo like that going to the bottom!"

To the Captain's great relief the lobsters at this moment created a diversion. He had dropped them on the hearth when he came in, and they were now clattering briskly about the room, butting into anything that came in their way in an effort to escape. He made a sudden dash after them and held them out toward Goodwife Pepperell.

28

"Here they be, ma'am," he said. "I'd saved them for my supper, and I'd take it kindly if ye'd cook them for me, and help eat them, too. It's raining cats and dogs, and if I was to start out now, I'd have a hard time finding the Lucy Ann. Ye can't see a rod ahead of ye in such a downpour."

"We shall be glad to have thee stay as long as thou wilt," said the Goodwife heartily. "Put the lobsters in this while I set the kettle to boil." She held out a wooden puncheon as she spoke, and the Captain dropped them in. Then he sat down with Goodman Pepperell on the settle beside the fireplace, and the two men talked of their boyhood in England, while she hung the kettle on the crane over the fire and began to prepare the evening meal.

"Daniel, sit thee down by the fire and get a good bed of coals ready while I mix the johnny-cake," she said as she stepped briskly about the room, and Daniel, nothing loath, drew a stool to the Captain's side and fed the fire with chips and corn-cobs

while he listened with all his ears to the talk of the two men.

"Well, Thomas, how hast thou prospered since I saw thee last?" asked Goodman Pepperell.

"Tolerable, tolerable, Josiah," answered the Captain. "I 've been mining for sea gold." Daniel wondered what in the world sea gold might be. "Ye see," he went on, turning to include Daniel in the conversation, "my father was a sea captain before me, and my gran'ther too. Why, my gran'ther helped send the Spanish Armada to the bottom where it belonged. Many and many's the time I've heard him tell about it, and I judge from what he said he must have done most of the job himself, though I reckon old Cap'n Drake may have helped some." (Here the Captain chuckled.) "He never came back from his last voyage, — overhauled by pirates more 'n likely. That was twenty years ago, and I've been following the sea myself ever since. I was wrecked off the Spanish Main on my first voyage, and I've run afoul of pirates and come near walking the plank more times than one, I'm telling ye, but somehow I always had the luck to get away! And here I be, safe and sound."

At this point the lobsters made a commotion in the wooden puncheon, and the Captain turned his attention to them. "Jest

31

spilin' to get out, ain't ye?" he inquired genially. "Look here, boy," to Daniel, "that water 's bilin'. Heave 'em in."

Daniel held his squirming victims over the pot, and not without a qualm of pity dropped them into the boiling water. Then he ventured to ask a question. "What is sea gold, Captain Sanders?"

"Things like them," answered the Captain, jerking his thumb at the lobsters, which were already beginning to turn a beautiful red color as they boiled in the pot; "as good gold as any that was ever dug out of mines ye can get for fish, and there never was such fishing in all the seas as there is along this coast! My! my! I 've seen schools of cod off the Cape making a solid floor of fish on the water so ye could walk on it if ye were so minded, and as for lobsters, I 've caught 'em that measured six and seven feet long! Farther down the coast there are oysters so big one of 'em will make a square meal for four or five people. It 's the truth I 'm telling ye."

Goodman Pepperell smiled. "Thomas," he said, "thou hast not lost thy power of narration!"

Captain Sanders for an instant looked a bit dashed, then he said, "Well, believe it or not, Josiah, it's the truth for all that. Why, talk about the land of Canaan flowin' with milk and honey! This here water's just alive with money! Any boy could go out and haul up a shilling on his own hook any time he liked."

Daniel, his eyes shining and his lips parted, was just making up his mind that he would rather be the captain of a fishing-smack than anything else in the world, since he knew he couldn't be a pirate, when his mother came to the fireplace with a layer of corn-meal dough spread on a baking-board. She placed the board in a slanting position against an iron trivet before the glowing bed of coals, and set a pot of beans in the ashes to warm. "Keep an eye on that johnny-cake," she said to Daniel, "and don't let it burn." Then she turned away to set the table.

This task took but little time, for in those days there were few things to put on it. She spread a snowy cloth of homespun linen on the plank which served as a table, and laid a knife and spoon at each place: there were no forks, and for plates only a

square of wood with a shallow depression
in the middle. Beside each of these trenchers she placed a napkin and a mug, and at
the Captain's place, as a special honor, she
set a beautiful tankard of wrought silver.
It was one of the few valuable things she
had brought with her from her English
home, and it was used only on great occa-
sions.

When these preparations were complete,
she took the lobsters from the pot, poured
the beans into a pewter dish, heaped the
golden johnny-cake high upon a trencher,
and, sending Dan to fetch Nancy, called
the men to supper. The storm was over by
this time, the last rays of the setting sun
were throwing long shadows over the fields,
and the robins were singing their evening
song. The Goodwife stepped to the window
and threw open the wooden shutters. "See,"
she said. "There's a rainbow."

"The sign of promise," murmured Goodman Pepperell, rising and looking over his
wife's shoulder.

"Fine day to-morrow," said the Captain. "Maybe I can plant my lobster-pots after all."

Nancy, looking pale and a little subdued, crept down the ladder and took her place with Daniel at the foot of the board. Then they all stood, while Goodman Pepperell asked a blessing on the food, and thanked God for his mercy in delivering them from danger and bringing them together in health and safety to partake of his bounty.

II
TWO DAYS

II

TWO DAYS

THE grace finished (it was a very long one and the beans were nearly cold before he said amen), Goodman Pepperell broke open the lobsters and piled the trenchers with johnny-cake and beans, and the whole family fell to with a right good will. All but Nancy. She was still a bit upset and did not feel hungry.

"Thou hast not told me, Captain, what voyage thou art about to undertake next," said the Goodman, sucking a lobster-claw with relish.

The Captain loved to talk quite as well as he loved to eat, but his mouth was full at this moment, and he paused before replying. "I'm getting too old for long voyages, Josiah," he said at last with a sigh. "Kind o' losing my taste for adventure. Pirates is

pretty plentiful yet, and for all I 'm a sailor
I 'd like to die in my bed, so I have settled
at Marblehead. They 're partial to fisher-
men along this coast. The town gives 'em
land for drying their fish and exempts 'em
from military dooty. But I can't stay ashore
a great while before my sea legs begin to
hanker for the feel of the deck rolling under
'em, so I 'm doing a coasting trade all up
and down the length of Massachusetts Bay.
I keep a parcel of lobster-pots going, some
here and some Plymouth way, and sell
them and fish, besides doing a carrying
trade for all the towns along-shore. It 's a
tame kind o' life. There, now," he finished,
"that 's all there is to say about me, and
I 'll just take a turn at these beans and give
ye a chance to tell about yourself, Josiah."

"'T is but a short tale," answered the
Goodman. "God hath prospered me. I
have an hundred acres of good farm land
along this river, and I have a cow, and a
flock of sheep to keep us in wool for the
Goodwife to spin. I have set out apple

trees, and there is wood for the cutting; the forest furnishes game and the sea is stored with food for our use; but the truth is there is more to do than can be compassed with one pair of hands. The neighbors help each other with clearing the land, log-rolling, building walls, and such as that, but if this country is to be developed we must do more than make a living. There are a thousand things calling to be done if there were but the men to do them."

The Captain skillfully balanced a mouthful of beans on his knife as he considered the problem. Finally he said, "Well, here's Dan'el, and, judging by the way he waded right into the tide after his sister, I calculate he'd be a smart boy to have round."

"He is," said the Goodman, and Daniel blushed to his eyes, for his father seldom praised him, "but he is not yet equal to a man's work, and moreover I want him to get some schooling. The Reverend John Harvard hath promised his library and quite a sum of money to found a college for the

41

training of ministers right here in Cambridge. The hand of the Lord hath surely guided us to this place, where he may receive an education, and it may even be that Daniel will be a minister, for the Colony sorely needs such."

"There, now," said the Captain. "Farming ain't such plain sailing; is it? Have ye thought of getting an Indian slave to help ye?"

"Truly I have thought of that," said the Goodman, "but they are a treacherous lot and passing lazy. There was a parcel of Pequot women and girls brought up from beyond Plymouth way last year after the uprising. The settlers had killed off all the men and sold the boys in the Bermudas. I might have bought one of the women but I need a man, or at least a boy that will grow into one. The Pequots are about all gone now, but the Narragansetts are none too friendly. They helped fight the Pequots because they hate them worse than they hate the English, but they are only biding their time, and some day it's likely we shall have trouble with them. Nay, I could never trust an Indian slave. Roger Williams saith they are wolves with men's brains, and he speaks the truth."

"Well, then," said the Captain, "why don't ye get a black? They are more docile than Indians, and the woods about are not full of their friends."

"Aye," agreed the Goodman, "the plan is a good one and well thought out, but they are hard to come by. There are only a few, even in Boston."

"There will soon be more, I'm thinking," said the Captain. "A ship was built in Marblehead last year on purpose for the trade. Captain Pierce is a friend of mine, and he's due at Providence any time now with a cargo of blacks from Guinea. Ye could sail down the bay with me, and there's a trail across the neck of the Cape to Providence, where the Desire will come to port. I expect to spend the Sabbath here, but I lift anchor on Monday. Ye can tell Captain

43

Pierce ye 're a friend of mine, and 't will do
ye no harm."

"Oh, Father," breathed Dan, "may I go,
too?"

The Captain chuckled. "Art struck with
the sea fever, son?" he said, looking down
into the boy's eager face. "Well, there's
room aboard. I might take ye along if so
be thy parents are willing and thou art
minded to see a bit of the world."

Up to this time Goodwife Pepperell had said no word, but now she spoke. "Are there not dangers enough on land without courting the dangers of the sea?" she asked.

Her husband looked at her with gentle disapproval. "Hold thy peace," he said. "What hath a pioneer lad to do with fear? Moreover, if he goes I shall be with him."

Nancy leaned forward and gazed imploringly at the Captain. "Dost thou not need some one to cook on thy boat?" she gasped. "I know well how to make johnny-cake and I —" then, seeing her father's stern look and her mother's distress, she wilted like a flower on its stem and was silent. The Captain smiled at her.

"Ye 're a fine cook, I make no doubt," he said genially, "but ye would n't go and leave Mother here all alone, now, I 'll be bound!"

"Nay," said Nancy faintly, looking at her mother.

Then the Goodwife spoke. "It pains me," she said, "to think of children torn

45

from their parents and sold into slavery, even though they be but Indians or blacks. I doubt not they have souls like ourselves."

"Read thy Bible, Susanna," answered her husband. "Cursed be Canaan. A servant of servants shall he be unto his brethren—thus say the Scriptures."

"Well, now," broke in the Captain, "if they have souls, they've either got to save 'em or lose 'em as I jedge it; and if they never have a chance to hear the Plan of Salvation, they're bound to be lost anyway. Bringin' 'em over here gives them their only chance to escape damnation, according to my notion."

"Hast thou ever brought over a cargo of slaves thyself?" asked the Goodwife.

"Nay," admitted the Captain, "but I sailed once on a slaver, and I own I liked not to see the poor critters when they were lured away. It seemed they could n't rightly sense that 't was for their eternal welfare, and I never felt called to set their feet in the way of Salvation by that means myself. I reckon I 'm not more than chicken-hearted, if ye come to that."

The meal was now over, the dusk had deepened as they lingered about the table, and Goodwife Pepperell rose to light a bay-berry candle and set it on the chimney-piece.

"Sit ye down by the fire again, while Nancy and I wash the dishes," she said cordially.

"Thank ye kindly," said the Captain, "but I must budge along. It's near dark, and Timothy — that's my mate — will be wondering if I 've been et up by a shark. It's going to be a clear night after the storm."

The children slept so soundly after the adventures of the day that their mother called them three times from the foot of the ladder in the early dawn of the following morning without getting any response. Then she mounted to the loft and shook Daniel gently. "Wake thee," she said. "'T is long past cock-crow, and Saturday at that."

Daniel opened his eyes feebly and was off to sleep again at once. "Daniel," she said, shaking him harder, "thy father is minded to take thee to Plymouth."

Before the words were fairly out of her mouth Daniel had popped out of bed as if he had been shot from a gun. "Oh, Mother," he shouted, "am I really to go? Shall I go clear to Providence? Doth Captain Sanders know? When do we start?"

"Thy father arranged it with the Captain last night," answered his mother. "He will come for thee in the little boat on Monday morning and will row thee and thy father to the sloop, which will sail at high tide. While thy father makes the journey across the Cape thou wilt go on to Provincetown with the Captain, or mayhap, if visitors are now permitted in the Colony, my aunt, the Governor's lady, will keep thee with her until thy father returns. She would like well to see my son, I know, and I trust thou wilt be a good lad and mind thy manners. Come, Nancy, child, I need thy help!"

Then she disappeared down the ladder to stir the hasty pudding, which was already bubbling in the pot.

When she was gone, Nancy flung herself upon the mattress and buried her face in the bed-clothes. "Oh, Daniel," she cried, smothering a sob, "what if the p-p-pirates should get thee?"

Daniel was at her side in an instant. "Give thyself no concern about pirates, sister," he said, patting her comfortingly. "I have thought how to deal with them! I shall stand by the rail with my cutlass in my hand, and when they seek to board her I will bring down my cutlass so,"—here he made a terrific sweep with his arm,—"and that will be the end of them."

"Oh," breathed Nancy, much impressed, "how brave thou art!"

"Well," said Daniel modestly, "there'd be the Captain and father to help, of course, and, I suppose, the mate too. There will be four of us men anyway."

"*Nancy! — Daniel!*" — it was their fa-

ther's voice this time, and the two children
jumped guiltily and began to dress as if the
house were on fire and they had but two
minutes to escape. In a surprisingly short
time they were downstairs and attending to
their morning tasks. Nancy, looking very
solemn, fed the chickens, and Dan brought
water from the spring, while their father
milked the cow; and by six o'clock their
breakfast of hasty pudding and milk had
been eaten, prayers were over, and the
whole family was ready for the real work
of the day. There was a great deal of it to
do, for nothing but "works of necessity and
mercy" could be performed on the Sabbath,
the Sabbath began at sundown Saturday
afternoon, and the travellers were to make
an early start on Monday morning. A fire
was built in the brick oven beside the fireplace, and while it was heating the Goodwife made four pies and six loaves of brown-
bread, and prepared a pot of pork and beans
for baking.

When the coals had been raked out and

the oven filled, she washed clothes for Daniel and his father, while Nancy hurried to
finish a pair of stockings she was knitting
for her brother. Daniel himself, meanwhile,
had gone down to the bay to see if he could
find the shovel and the basket. He came

home in triumph about noon with both, and with quite a number of clams beside, which the Goodwife cooked for their dinner. When they were seated at the table, and the Goodman had asked the blessing, he leaned back in his chair and surveyed the ceiling of the cabin. From the rafters there hung long festoons of dried pumpkin and golden ears of corn. There were also sausages, hams, and sides of bacon.

"I doubt not you will fare well while we are gone," he said. "There is plenty of well-cured meat, and meal enough ground to last for some time. The planting is done and the corn well hoed; there is wood cut, and Gran'ther Wattles will call upon you if he knows I am away. I am leaving the fowling-piece for thee, wife. The musket I shall take with me."

"Why must Gran'ther Wattles come?" interrupted Nancy in alarm. "I am sure Mother and I do not need him."

"Children should be seen and not heard," said her father. "It is Gran'ther Wattles's duty to oversee the congregation at home as well as in the meeting-house."

Nancy looked at her trencher and said no more, but she thought there was already enough to bear without having Gran'ther Wattles added to her troubles. Daniel, meanwhile, had attacked his porringer of clams, and in his excitement over the journey was gobbling at a fearful rate. His mother looked at him despairingly.

"Daniel," she said, "thou art pitching food into thy mouth as if thou wert shoveling coals into the oven! Take thy elbows off the table and eat more moderately." Daniel glued his elbows to his side. "Sit up straight," she went on, "or thou wilt grow up as crooked as a ram's horn." Daniel immediately sat up as if he had swallowed the poker. "I wish thee to practice proper manners at home, lest my aunt should think thee a person of no gentility. Remember thou must not ask for anything at the table. Wait until it is offered thee, and then do not stuff it down as if thine eyes had not looked upon food for a fortnight!"

"But," protested poor Dan, who was beginning to feel that the journey might not be all his fancy had painted, "suppose they should n't offer it?"

"I do not fear starvation for thee," his mother answered briefly; "and oh, Daniel, I beg of thee to wash thy hands before going to the table! The Governor is a proper man and my aunt is very particular." She paused for breath, and to get more brownbread for the table.

When she sat down again, Daniel said, "If you please, I think I 'd rather go on to Provincetown with the Captain."

"That must be as we are guided at the time," said his father.

The busy day passed quickly, and before sunset a fine array of pies and brown loaves were cooling on the table, the chores were done, and a Sabbath quiet had settled down over the household, not to be broken until sunset of the following day.

When Daniel opened the cabin door the next morning, he was confronted by a wall of gray mist which shut the landscape entirely from view. He had hoped to catch a glimpse of the Lucy Ann, in order to assure himself that he had not merely dreamed the events of the day before, but nothing could he see, and he began dispirited preparations for church. They had no clock, and on account of the fog they could not tell the time by the sun, so the whole family started early to cross the long stretch of pasture land which lay between them and the meeting-house in the village. They reached it just as Gran'ther Wattles, looking very grave and important, came out on the church steps and beat a solemn tattoo upon a drum to call the people together. They came from different directions across the fields and through the one street of the village, looking anxious for fear they should be late, yet not daring to desecrate the Sabbath by any appearance of haste. Among the rest, red-faced and short of wind, who should appear but Captain Sanders? Sabbath decorum forbade any show of surprise; so Goodman Pepperell and his wife merely bowed gravely, and the Captain, looking fairly pop-eyed in his effort to keep properly solemn, nodded in return, and they passed into the meeting-house together.

The Captain sat down with the Goodman on the men's side of the room, while Daniel went to his place among the boys, leaving Nancy and his mother seated with the women on the opposite side. It is hard to believe that a boy could sit through a sermon two hours long with his friends all about him and such a secret buttoned up inside his jacket without an explosion, but Daniel did it. He did n't dare do otherwise, for Gran'ther Wattles ranged up and down the little aisle with his tithing-rod in hand on the lookout for evil-doers. Once, indeed, during the sermon there was a low rumbling snore, and Daniel was horrified to see Gran'ther Wattles lean over and gently tickle the Captain's nose with the squirrel-

tail. The Captain woke with a start and
sneezed so violently that the boy next Daniel all but tittered outright. Gran'ther Wattles immediately gave him a smart rap on
the head with the knob end of his stick, so
it is no wonder that after that Daniel sat
with his eyes nearly crossed in his effort to
keep them fixed on the minister, though his
thoughts were far away ranging Massachusetts Bay with the Lucy Ann of Marblehead.

At last, however, the sermon ended, the
final psalm was sung, and after the benedic-
tion the minister passed out of the church
and the congregation dispersed to eat a bite
of brown-bread in the church-yard before
assembling again for another two-hour sermon.

The sun was now shining brightly, and,
once outside the door, after the first sermon, the Captain wiped his brow as if exhausted, and a few moments later Daniel
saw him quietly disappearing in the direction of the river. He was not of the Cam-

bridge parish, so no discipline could be
exercised upon him, but Gran'ther Wattles
set him down at once as a dangerous char-
acter, and even Goodwife Pepperell shook
her head gently when she noted his absence.

Somehow, although it was a breach of

Sabbath decorum to tell it, the great news leaked out during the intermission, and Daniel was the center of interest to every boy in the congregation during the afternoon. When the second long sermon was over and the exhausted minister had trailed solemnly down the aisle, the equally exhausted people walked sedately to their houses, discussing the sermon as they went. All that day Daniel kept a tight clutch on his manners, but the moment the sun went down, he heaved a great sigh of relief and turned three somersaults and a handspring behind the cabin to limber himself up after the fearful strain.

III
ON BOARD THE LUCY ANN

III

ON BOARD THE LUCY ANN

THE family rose at daybreak the next morning, tasks were quickly performed, and after
breakfast the Goodman read a chapter in
the Bible and prayed long and earnestly
that God would bless their journey, protect
those who were left behind, and bring them
all together again in safety. Then he and
Daniel started down the path to the river,
with Nancy and her mother, both looking
very serious, following after. The tide was
already coming in, and the bay stretched before them a wide sheet of blue water spar-
kling in the sun. In the distance they could
see the sails of the Lucy Ann being hoisted
and Captain Sanders in his small boat row-
ing rapidly toward the landing-place.

"Ship ahoy!" shouted Daniel, waving
his cap as the boat approached.

"Ahoy, there!" answered the Captain, and in a moment the keel grated on the sand, and the Goodman turned to his wife and daughter.

"The Lord watch between me and thee while we are absent one from the other," he said reverently, and "Amen!" boomed the Captain. Then there were kisses and good-byes, and soon Nancy and her mother were alone on the shore, waving their hands until the boat was a mere speck on the dancing blue waters. As it neared the Lucy Ann, they went back to the cabin, and there they watched the white sails gleaming in the sun until they disappeared around a headland.

"Come, Nancy," said her mother when the ship was quite out of sight, "idleness will only make loneliness harder to bear. Here is a task for thee." She handed her a basket of raw wool. "Take this and card it for me to spin."

Nancy hated carding with all her heart, but she rose obediently, brought the basket

64

to the doorway, and, sitting down in the sunshine, patiently carded the wool into little wisps ready to be wound on a spindle and spun into yarn by the mother's skillful hands.

Meanwhile Daniel was standing on the deck of the Lucy Ann, drinking in the fresh salt breeze and eagerly watching the shores as the boat passed between Charlestown and Boston and dropped anchor in the harbor to set the Captain's lobster-pots. All the wonderful bright day they sailed past rocky islands and picturesque headlands, with the Captain at the tiller skillfully keeping the vessel to the course and at the same time spinning yarns to Daniel and his father about the adventures which had overtaken him at various points along the coast. At Governor's Island he had caught a giant lobster. He had been all but wrecked in a fog off Thompson's Island.

"Ye see that point of land," he said, waving his hand toward a rocky promontory extending far out into the bay. "That's

65

Squantum. Miles Standish of Plymouth named it that after an Indian that was a good friend of the Colony in the early days. Well, right off there I was overhauled by a French privateer once. 'Privateer' is a polite name for a pirate ship. She was loaded with molasses, indigo, and such from the West Indies, and I had a cargo of beaver-skins. If it had n't been that her sailors was mostly roarin' drunk at the time, it 's likely that would have been the end of Thomas Sanders, skipper, sloop, and all, but my boat was smaller and quicker than theirs, and, knowing these waters so well, I was able to give 'em the slip and get out into open sea; and here I be! Ah, those were the days!"

The Captain heaved a heavy sigh for the lost joys of youth and was silent for a moment. Then his eyes twinkled and he began another story. "One day as we was skirtin' the shores of Martha's Vineyard," he said, "we were followed by a shark. Now, there 's nothing a sailor hates worse than

66

a shark; and for good reasons. They're the pirates of the deep; that's what they are. They'll follow a vessel for days, snapping up whatever the cook throws out, and hoping somebody'll fall overboard to give 'em a full meal. Well, sir, there was a sailor aboard on that voyage that had a special grudge against sharks. He'd been all but et up by one once, and he allowed this was his chance to get even; so he let out a hook baited with a whole pound of salt pork, and the shark gobbled it down instanter, hook and all. They hauled him up the ship's side, and then that sailor let himself down over the rails by a rope, and cut a hole in the shark's gullet, or whatever they call the pouch the critter carries his supplies in, and took out the pork. Then he dropped him back in the water and threw the pork in after him. Well, sir, believe it or not, that shark sighted the pork bobbing round in the water; so he swallowed it again. Of course it dropped right out through the hole in his gullet, and, by jolly! as long as

67

we could see him that shark was continuing to swallow that piece of pork over and over again. I don't know as I ever see any animal get more pleasure out of his rations than that shark got out of that pound of pork. I believe in bein' kind to dumb critters," he finished, "and I reckon the shark is about the dumbdest there is. Anyhow that one surely did die happy." Here the Captain solemnly winked his eye.

"What became of the sailor?" asked Dan.

"That sailor was me," admitted the Captain. "That's what became of him, and served him right, too."

They slept that night on the deck of the sloop, and before light the next morning Dan was awakened by the groaning of the chain as the anchor was hauled up, and the flapping of the sails as Timothy hoisted them to catch a stiff breeze which was blowing from the northeast. The second day passed like the first. The weather was fine, the winds favorable, and that evening they rounded Duxbury Point and entered Plymouth Bay just as the sun sank behind the hills back of the town.

"Here's the spot where the Mayflower dropped anchor," said the Captain, as the sloop approached a strip of sandy beach stretching like a long finger into the water. "I generally bring the Lucy Ann to at the same place. She can't go out again till high tide to-morrow, for the harbor is shallow and we'd likely run aground; so ye'll have the whole morning to spend with your relations, and that's more than I'd want to spend with some of mine, I'm telling ye," and he roared with laughter. "Relations is like victuals," he went on. "Some agrees with ye, and some don't."

"Our relations are the Bradfords," said Goodman Pepperell with dignity.

"And a better man than the Governor never trod shoe-leather," said the Captain heartily. "He and Captain Standish and Mr. Brewster and Edward Winslow—why, those four men have piloted this town

69

through more squalls than would overtake most places in a hundred years! If anything could kill 'em they would have been under ground years ago. They 've had starvation and Indians and the plague followin' after 'em like a school of sharks ever since they dropped anchor here well nigh on to twenty years ago, and whatever happens they just thank the Lord as if 't was a special blessing and go right along! By jolly!" declared the Captain, blowing his nose violently, "they nigh about beat old Job for patience! 'Though He slay me, yet will I trust in Him,' says old Job, but his troubles was all over after a bit, and he got rewarded with another full set of wives and children and worldly goods, so he could see plain as print that righteousness paid. But these men, — their reward for trouble is just more trouble, fer 's I can see. They surely do beat all for piety."

"'Whom the Lord loveth He chasteneth,'" quoted the Goodman.

"The Lord must be mighty partial to

Plymouth, then," answered the Captain as he brought the sloop gently round the point, "for she's been shown enough favor to spile her, according to my way of thinkin'."

It was too late to go ashore that night, and from the deck Dan watched the stars come out over the little village, not dreaming that it held in its humble keeping the brave spirit of a great nation that was to be.

When Daniel opened his eyes next morning, his father and the Captain were already stowing various packages in the small boat, and from the tiny forecastle came an appetizing smell of frying fish.

"Here ye be," said the Captain cheerily to Dan, "bright as a new shilling and ready to eat I'll be bound. As soon as we've had a bite we'll go ashore. I've got to row clear over to Duxbury after I do my errands in Plymouth, but I'll hunt ye up when I get back. Nobody can get lost in this town without he goes out of it! I could spot ye from the deck most anywhere on the map. Then, my lad, if your father says the word, I'll bring ye back to the Lucy Ann while he goes across the neck. Ye'll get a taste of mackerel-fishing if ye come along o' me. Ye can make yourself handy on deck and keep a quarter of your own catch for yourself if you're lively. A tub of salt fish would be a tidy present to your mother when you get back home."

"Oh, I want to go with you," cried Daniel, remembering with terror what was expected of him in the way of manners should he be invited to stay at the Governor's. He looked questioningly at his father, but was answered only by a grave smile, and he knew better than to plead.

" Here, now," cried the Captain, as Timothy appeared with a big trencher of smoking fish and corn bread, " tie up to the dock and stow away some of this cargo in your insides."

Neither Daniel nor his father needed a second invitation, for the keen salt air had given them the appetite of wolves, and the breakfast was soon disposed of according to directions. Then the two followed the Captain over the side and into the boat, which had been lowered and was now bobbing about on the choppy waves of the bay. When they were settled and the boat was properly trimmed, the Captain rowed toward a small stream of clear water which flowed down from the hills back of the town, and landed them at the foot of the one little

street of the village. The Captain drew the
boat well up on the shore and stowed letters and parcels in various places about his
person, and the three started up the hill

74

together. They had not gone far, when a childish voice shouted, "There's Captain Sanders," and immediately every child within hearing came tumbling down the hill till they swarmed about him like flies about a honey-pot.

"Pirates!" cried the Captain, holding up his hands in mock terror. "I surrender. Come aboard and seize the cargo!" He held open the capacious pocket which hung from his belt, and immediately half a dozen small hands plunged into it and came out laden with raisins.

"Here, now, divide fairly," shouted the Captain. "No pigs!" and with children clinging to his hands and coat-tails he made a slow progress up the hill, Daniel and his father following closely in his wake.

As they were nearing the Common House, two more children caught sight of him and came racing to meet him. The Captain dived into his pocket for more raisins and found it empty, but he was equal to the emergency. "Here, you, Mercy and

75

Joseph Bradford," he cried, " I 've brought
you something I have n't brought to any one
else. I 've brought you a new cousin." The
other children had been so absorbed in their
old friend they had scarcely noticed the
strangers hitherto, but now they turned to
gaze curiously at Daniel and his father.
Joseph and Mercy were both a little younger
than Daniel, and all three were shy, but no
one could stay shy long when the Captain
was about, and soon they were walking
along together in the friendliest manner.

"Where 's thy father, young man?" said
the Captain, speaking to Joseph. " I have
a letter for him, and I have brought a rela-
tion for him too."

" I wish you would bring me a cousin,"
said one little girl enviously.

" Well, now," roared the Captain, "think
of that! I have a few relations of my own
left over that I 'd be proper glad to parcel
out amongst ye if I 'd only known ye was
short, but I have n't got 'em with me."

"Father 's in there," said Joseph, point-

ing to the Common House. "They're having a meeting. Elder Brewster's there, too,
and Mr. Winslow and Captain Standish
and Governor Prence." It was evident that
some matter of importance was being dis-
cussed, for a little knot of women had gathered before the door as if waiting for some
decision to be announced.

They had almost reached the group,
when suddenly from the north there came
a low roaring noise, and the earth beneath
their feet shook and trembled so violently
that many of the children were thrown to
the ground, while the bundles Goodman
Pepperell was carrying for the Captain flew
in every direction. Those who kept their
feet at all reeled and staggered in a strange,
wild dance, and every child in the group
screamed with all his might. The women
screamed, too, calling frantically to the
children, and the men came pouring out of
the door of the Common House, trying to
steady themselves as they were flung first
one way, then another by the heaving

ground. It lasted but a few dreadful moments, and the Captain was the first to recover his speech.

"There, now," said he, a little breathlessly, "ain't it lucky I had my sea legs on ! 'T wa'n't anything but an earthquake, anyway."

The instant they could stay on their feet, the children ran to their mothers, who were also running to them, and in less time than it takes to tell it the whole village was gathered before the Common House. As Daniel, with the Captain and his father, joined the stricken company, Governor Bradford was speaking. He had been Governor of the Colony for so long that in time of sudden stress the people still turned to him for counsel though Mr. Prence was really the Governor.

"Think ye not that the finger of the Lord would direct us by this visitation?" he said to the white-faced group. "We were met together in council because some of our number wish to go away from Plymouth to find broader pastures for their cattle, even as Jacob separated from Esau with all his flocks and herds. In this I see a sign of God's displeasure at our removals one from another."

John Howland now found his voice. "Nay, but," he said, "shall we limit the bounty of the Lord and say, 'Only here shall He prosper us'?"

"What say the Scriptures to him who was not content with abundance, but must tear down his barns to build bigger?" answered the Governor. "'This night thy soul shall be required of thee.'"

There was no reply, and the pale faces grew a shade paler as a second rumble was heard in the distance, the earth again began to tremble, and a mighty wave, rolling in from the sea, crashed against the shore. Above the noise of the waters rose the voice of Governor Bradford. "He looketh upon the earth and it trembleth. He toucheth the hills and they smoke. The Lord is merciful and gracious. He will not always chide, neither will He keep his anger forever. He hath not dealt with us after our sins."

Seeing how frightened the people were, the Captain broke the silence which fell upon the trembling group after the Governor's words. "Lord love ye!" he cried heartily. "This wa'n't no earthquake to speak of. 'T wa'n't scarcely equal to an ague chill down in the tropics! They would n't have no respect for it down there. 'T would n't more than give 'em an appetite for their victuals."

His laugh which followed cheered many hearts, and was echoed in faint smiles on the pale faces of the colonists. Governor Bradford himself smiled and, turning to the Captain, held out his hand. "Thou art ever a tonic, Thomas," he said, "and there is always a welcome for thee in Plymouth and for thy friends, too," he added, turning to the Goodman.

"Though thou knowest him not, he is haply more thy friend than mine," said the Captain, pushing the Goodman and Daniel forward to shake hands with the Governor. "He is married to Mistress Bradford's niece and his name is Pepperell."

"Josiah Pepperell, of Cambridge?" said the Governor's lady, coming forward to welcome him.

"At your service, madam," answered the Goodman, bowing low, "and this is my son Daniel."

Daniel bowed in a manner to make his mother proud of him if she could have seen him, and then Mercy and Joseph swarmed up, bringing their older brother William, a lad of fifteen, to meet his new cousin, and the four children ran away together, all their tongues wagging briskly about the exciting event of the day. The earthquake had now completely passed, and the people, roused from their terror, hastened to their homes to repair such damage as had been done and to continue the tasks which it had interrupted. Meanwhile the Captain distributed his letters and parcels, leaving the Governor to become acquainted with his new relative, learn his errand, and help him on his journey, while his wife hastened home to prepare a dinner for company.

It was a wonderful dinner that she set before them. There were succotash and baked codfish, a good brown loaf, and pies made of blueberries gathered and dried the summer before. Oh, if only Daniel's mother could have been there to see his table manners on that occasion! He sat up as straight as a ramrod, said "please" and "thank you," ate in the most genteel manner possible, even managing blueberry pie without disaster, and was altogether such an example of behavior that Mistress Bradford said before the meal was half over, "Thou 'lt leave the lad with us, Cousin Pepperell, whilst thou art on thy journey?"

"I fear to trouble thee," said the Goodman. "And the Captain hath a purpose to take him to Provincetown and meet me here on my return."

"The land is mayhap safer than the sea should another earthquake visit us," said the Governor gravely, "and he will more than earn his keep if he will but help William with the corn and other tasks. Like thyself we are in sad need of more hands."

Daniel looked eagerly at his father, for he already greatly admired his cousin William and longed to stay with him. Moreover, the earthquake had somewhat modified his appetite for adventure.

"His eyes plead," said the Goodman, "and I know it would please his mother. So by your leave he may stay."

A whoop of joy from the three young Bradfords was promptly suppressed by their mother. "For shame!" she said. "Thy cousin Daniel will think thou hast learned thy manners from the savages. Thou shouldst take a lesson from his behavior."

Poor Daniel squirmed on his stool and thought if he must be an example every moment of his stay he would almost choose being swallowed up by a tidal wave at sea after all. The matter had been settled, however, and that very afternoon the Goodman set off on a hired horse, with his musket across his saddle-bow, and a head full of instructions from the Governor about the dangers of the road, and houses where he might spend the nights.

There was a queer lump in Daniel's throat as he caught the last glimpse of his father's sturdy back as it disappeared down the forest trail, and that night, when he went to bed with William in the loft of the Governor's log house, he thought long and tenderly of his mother and Nancy. If he had only had a magic mirror such as Beauty had in the palace of the Beast, he might have looked into it and seen them going patiently about their daily tasks with nothing to break the monotonous routine of work except a visit from Gran'ther Wattles, who came to see if Nancy knew her catechism. The earthquake had been felt there so very slightly that they did not even know there had been one, until the Captain stopped on his return voyage the next week to bring them word of the safe journey to Plymouth.

IV
A FOREST TRAIL

IV

A FOREST TRAIL

To Daniel the days of his stay in Plymouth passed quickly. He hoed corn with his cousin William and pulled weeds in the garden with Joseph and Mercy, and in the short hours allowed them for play there was always the sea. They ran races on the sand when the tide was out and were never tired of searching for the curious things washed ashore by the waves. One day they gathered driftwood and made a fire on the shore, hung a kettle over it and cooked their own dinner of lobsters fresh from the water. Another day William and Daniel went together in a rowboat nearly to Duxbury, and caught a splendid codfish that weighed ten pounds. On another wonderful day John Howland took the two boys hunting with him. It was the first time Daniel had ever been allowed to carry a gun quite like a man, and he was the proudest lad in all Plymouth that night when the three hunters returned bringing with them two fine wild turkeys, and a hare which Daniel had shot. He loved the grave, wise, kindly Governor and his brave wife, and grew to know, by sight at least, most of the other people of the town.

More than ten days passed in this way, and they were beginning to wonder why the Goodman did not return. The Captain had come back from Provincetown and had been obliged to go on to Boston without waiting for him, and there was no knowing when the Lucy Ann would appear again in Plymouth Harbor. Then one day, as Dan and William were working in the corn-field, they saw a tired horse with two people on his back come out of the woods. Daniel took a long look at the riders, then, throwing down his hoe and shouting, "It's Father!" tore off at top speed to meet him. William picked up his hoe and followed at a slower pace. When he reached the group,

Dan was up behind his father on the pillion with his arms about him, and standing before them on the ground was a black boy about William's own size and age. He had only a little ragged clothing on, and what he had seemed to make him uneasy, perhaps because he had been used to none at all in his native home far across the sea. His eyes were rolling wildly from one face to another, and it was plain that he was in a great state of fear.

"He is but a savage as yet," said Goodman Pepperell. " He was doubtless roughly handled on the voyage and hath naught but fear and hatred in his heart. It will take some time to make a Christian of him! Thou must help in the task, Daniel, for thou art near his age and can better reach his darkened mind. As yet he understands but one thing. He can eat like a Christian, or rather like two of them ! We must tame him with food and kindness."

"What is his name ?" asked Daniel, still gazing at the boy with popping eyes, for

never before had he seen a skin so dark.

"Call him Zeb," said his father.

"Come, Zeb," said William, taking the boy gently by the arm, and looking compassionately into the black face. "Food!" He shouted the word at him as if he were deaf, but poor Zeb, completely bewildered by these strange, meaningless sounds, only shrank away from him and looked about as if seeking a way of escape.

Daniel immediately sprang from the pillion and seized Zeb's other arm. "Yes, Zeb, *food—good*," he howled, pointing down his own throat and rubbing his stomach with an ecstatic expression. It is probable that poor Zeb understood from this pantomime that he was about to be eaten alive, for he made a furious effort to get away. The boys held firmly to his arms, smiling and nodding at him in a manner meant to be reassuring, but which only convinced the poor black that they were pleased with the tenderness of his flesh and were enjoying the prospect of a cannibal feast. With the slave boy between them, "hanging back and digging in his claws like a cat being pulled by the tail," as Dan told his mother afterward, they made slow progress toward the village.

News of the return spread quickly, and a curious crowd of children gathered to gaze at Zeb, for many of them had never seen a negro before in their lives. Goodman Pepperell went at once to the Governor's house, and when he learned that the Captain had come and gone, he decided to push on to Boston at once by land. "'T is an easier journey than the one I have just taken," he said. "There are settlements along the way, and time passes. I have been gone now longer than I thought. The farm work waits, and Susanna will fear for our safety. I must start home as soon as I can return this horse to the owner and secure another. I would even buy a good mare, for I stand in need of one on my farm."

"At least thou must refresh thyself before starting," said the Governor's wife cordially, and she set about getting dinner at once.

While his father went with the Governor to make arrangements for the journey, Daniel and his cousins took charge of Zeb. With Mistress Bradford's permission they built a fire on the shore and cooked dinner there for themselves and the black boy, who was more of a show to them than a whole circus with six clowns would be to us. As he watched the boys lay the sticks and start the blaze, Zeb's eyes rolled more wildly than ever. No doubt he thought that he himself was to be roasted over the coals, and when at last he saw William lay a big fish on the fire instead, his relief was so great that for the first time he showed a row of gleaming teeth in a hopeful grin. Daniel brought him a huge piece of it when the fish was cooked, and from that moment Zeb regarded him as his friend.

It was early afternoon before all the preparations were completed and the little caravan was ready to start on its perilous journey. There were two horses, and John Howland, who knew the trail well and was wise in woodcraft, was to go with them as far as Marshfield, where he knew of a horse that was for sale. Half the town gathered to see them off. John Howland mounted first, and Daniel was placed on the pillion behind him. Then Zeb was made to get up behind the Goodman, and off they started, followed by a volley of farewells and messages from the group of Plymouth friends left behind.

For a little distance they followed the shore-line, then, plunging into the woods, they were soon lost to view. The road was a mere blazed trail through dense forests, and it was necessary to keep a sharp lookout lest they lose their way and also because no traveler was for a moment safe from possible attack by Indians. Hour after hour they plodded patiently along, sometimes dismounting and walking for a mile or so to stretch their legs and rest the horses. There was little chance for talk, because the path was too narrow for them to go side by side. The day was warm, and if it had not been for slapping the mosquitoes which buzzed about them in swarms, Daniel would have fallen asleep sitting in the saddle. In the late afternoon, as they came out upon an open moor, Daniel was roused by hearing a suppressed exclamation from John Howland and felt him reach for the pistol which hung from his belt. His horse pricked up his ears and whinnied, and the horse on which the Goodman and Zeb were riding answered with a loud neigh. Daniel peered over John Howland's broad shoulder just in time to see a large deer disappearing into a thicket of young birches some distance ahead of them.

"Oh!" cried Daniel, pounding on John Howland's ribs in his excitement, "let's get him!"

"Not so fast, not so fast," said John in a low voice, pinning with his elbow the hand that was battering his side. "Let be! Thou hast seen but half. There was an Indian on the track of that deer. Should we step in and take his quarry, he might be minded to empty his gun into us instead! I saw him standing nigh the spot where the trail enters the wood again yonder, and when he saw us he slipped like a shadow into the underbrush."

He stopped his horse, the Goodman came alongside, and the two men talked together in a low tone. "Shall we go on as if we had not seen him?" asked the Goodman. John Howland considered.

"If we turn back, the savage will be persuaded we have seen him and are afraid," he said. "We must e'en take our chance. It may be he hath no evil intent, though the road be lonely and travelers few. Whatever his purpose, it is safer to go on than to stand still," and, tightening his rein, he boldly urged his horse across the open space.

Daniel's heart thumped so loudly against his ribs that it sounded to his ears like a drum-beat as they crossed the clearing and entered the forest on the other side. They had gone but a short distance into the woods when they were startled by the report of a gun, and poor Zeb fell off his horse and lay like one dead in the road. For a moment they thought he had been shot, and the two men were about to spring to his rescue, when Zeb scrambled to his feet and began to run like one possessed.

"He is but scared to death. Haply he hath never heard a gun go off before," said John Howland, and, sticking his spurs into his horse, he gave chase.

Fleet of foot though he was, Zeb was no match for a horse and was soon overtaken.

"'T was but the Indian shooting the deer," said John Howland, laughing in spite of himself at poor Zeb's wild-eyed terror. "'T is a promise of safety for the present at least. Nevertheless I like not the look of it. The red-skin saw us; make no doubt of that; for when I first beheld him he was peering at us as though to fix our faces in his mind."

" I, too, marked how he stared," answered the Goodman, as he seized the cowering Zeb and swung him again to his seat on the pillion.

"I have it," he said, stopping short as he was about to mount. "The savage is without doubt of the Narragansett tribe. He caught a glimpse of the dark skin of this boy and mistook him for an Indian lad — one of the hated Pequots, who they thought were either all dead or sold out of the country. 'T is likely they have no knowledge of other dark-skinned people than themselves."

"It may be so," said John Howland, doubtfully, "but 't is as likely they mistook him for a devil. It once befell that some Indians, finding a negro astray in the forest, were minded to destroy him by conjuring, thinking him a demon. To be sure 't is but a year since the Narragansetts helped the English destroy the Pequot stronghold, and the few Pequots who were neither killed nor sold they still hold in subjection. Whatever their idea, it bodes no good either to Zeb or to us, for their enmity never sleeps."

Zeb, meantime, sat clutching the pillion and looking from one grave face to the other as if he knew they were talking of him, and the Goodman patted his shoulder reassuringly as he mounted again. They were now nearing a small settlement, and the path widened so the two horses could walk abreast.

"Thou 'lt have a special care in the stretch from well beyond Mount Dagon," said John

Howland, "for thou knowest of the notorious Morton, who founded there the settlement called Merry Mount. It was the worshipful Endicott who wiped it out. Much trouble hath Morton to answer for. He hath corrupted the savages, adding his vices to theirs. He hath also sold them guns and taught them to use them, for which cause the Indians of this region are more to be feared than any along the coast. They are drunken, armed, and filled with hate for any whom they esteem their enemies."

Daniel's hair fairly stood on end. He had felt prepared for pirates, but Indians lurking in dark forests were quite another matter! He wished with all his heart that John Howland were going with them all the way to Cambridge, but he well knew that could not be. His spirits rose somewhat as they came in sight of the settlement, and a hearty supper at the house of Goodman Richards put such life and courage into his heart that before it was over the Indians were no more to him than pirates! Then, while his father

99

and John Howland arranged with Goodman Richards for the purchase of a horse
to take them the rest of their journey,
Goodwife Richards stowed Dan away in
an attic bed, while Zeb, worn out with
fear and fatigue, slept soundly on the
hearth.

Courage is always highest in the morning, and Daniel felt bold as a lion the next
day, as he and his father bade John Howland and the Richards family good-bye and,
with Zeb, again entered the forest trail. The
two boys walked on ahead, while the Goodman became acquainted with the new horse,
whose name, Goodman Richards had told
him, was Penitence, but which they short-
ened to Penny. Later, when he had assured
himself that the animal was trustworthy,
Goodman Pepperell put the two boys in
the saddle and walked beside them, leading
Penny by the bridle. Taking turns in this
way, they went on for some miles without
incident, until Dan almost forgot his fears,
and even Zeb — watching his face and echo-

ing its expression on his own — grew less
and less timid.

They had passed the place which Howland had called Mount Dagon and which
is now known as Wollaston, and had crossed
the Neponset River by a horse bridge and
were walking along quite cheerfully, the
two boys at some distance ahead of Penny,

when they saw a little way ahead of them an Indian standing motionless beside the trail. Dan immediately drew Zeb behind a bush, and when an instant later his father came up, the Indian disappeared as suddenly as he had come.

The Goodman looked troubled. "It is the same one we saw yesterday, I feel sure!" he said. "I like not his following us in this way, Daniel. I must trust thee even as though thou wert a man. Do thou get upon the horse's back with Zeb behind thee. I will walk ahead with my gun ready. Should the savage attack us, do thou speed thy horse like the wind to the next village, and bring back help. Remember it is thy part to obey. Three lives may hang on it."

With his heart pounding like a trip-hammer Dan mounted Penny. Zeb was placed on the pillion behind him with both arms clutching his waist, and the Goodman strode ahead, his keen eyes watching in every direction for any sign of danger. There was not a sound in the forest except the soft thud of the horse's feet, the cawing of a crow circling out of sight over the tree-tops, and the shrill cry of a blue jay.

"Confound thee, thou marplot, thou busy-body of the wood," muttered the Goodman to himself as he listened. "Wert thou but a human gossip, I'd set thee in the stocks till thou hadst learned to hold thine evil tongue!"

But the blue jay only kept up his squawk-ing, passing the news on to his brethren until the forest rang with word of their approach.

It did not need the blue jays to tell of their progress, however, for though no other sound had betrayed their advance, two In-dians were creeping stealthily through the underbrush, keeping pace with the travel-ers, and when they had reached a favor-able spot in a small clearing, they suddenly sprang from their hiding-place. With a blood-curdling cry they leaped forward, and, seizing one of Zeb's legs, tried to drag him from the horse's back.

The yells of the Indians were as nothing to those that Zeb then let loose! The air was fairly split by blood-curdling shrieks, and the horse, terrified in turn, leaped forward, tearing Zeb from the grasp of the Indian and almost unseating Dan by the jerk. But Dan dug his knees into the horse's sides, flung his arms about her neck, and, holding on for dear life, tore away up the trail with Zeb clinging like a limpet to his waist.

Never was a ride like that. Even John Gilpin's was a mild performance beside it, for Zeb shrieked every minute of the way as they sped along, with the horse's tail streaming out behind like the tail of a comet, and the daylight showing between the bouncing boys and Penny's back at every wild leap. Even if Daniel had not been minded to obey his father's command, he could not have helped himself, for Penny took matters into her own four hoofs, and never paused in her wild career until, covered with foam, she dashed madly into a little hamlet where the village of Neponset now stands.

Samuel Kittredge was just starting for

the forest with his axe on his shoulder, when his ears were smitten by the frantic shrieks of Zeb, and, thinking it must be a wildcat on the edge of the clearing, he started back to the house for his gun. Before he reached it, Penitence, with the two boys on her back, came thundering toward him at full gallop, and stopped at his side.

"What in tarnation is the matter with ye?" he exclaimed, gazing in amazement at the strange apparition. "I declare for it, that nigger is all but scared plumb white! What ails ye?"

"Indians!" gasped Dan, pointing toward the trail. "My father—quick!" No more words were needed. Samuel Kittredge dashed into his house, snatched his gun from the chimney, and, dashing out again, fired it into the air. Poor Zeb! He slid off over the horse's tail on to the ground and lay there in a heap, while a knot of men, responding to the signal of Sam Kittredge's gun, gathered hurriedly before his house and started at once down the trail.

"You stay here," said Sam to Dan as he started away. "We'll be back soon with your father if the pesky red-skins have n't got him."

"Or if they have," added another man grimly, and off they went.

Goodwife Kittredge now took charge of Dan and Zeb, while her son, a boy of eleven, tied Penny to a tree beside their cabin. Zeb recovered at once when she offered him a generous slice of brown-bread, but Dan was too anxious about his father to eat. He stood beside Penny, rubbing her neck and soothing her, with his eyes constantly on the trail and his ears eagerly listening for the sound of shots. It seemed an age, but really was not more than half an hour, before he saw the men come out of the woods, and, oh joy! his father was with them!

Leaving Penny nibbling grass, he ran to meet them and threw his arms about his father's neck, crying, "Oh, dear father, art thou hurt?"

"Nay; the Lord was merciful," answered the Goodman. "I fired but one shot, and hit one of the red-skins, I am sure, for they both dived back into the woods at once. I hid myself in the thick underbrush on the other side of the trail and waited, thinking perhaps I could creep along beside it out of sight, but Zeb's roaring must have frighted the Indians. Doubtless they knew it would rouse the countryside. At any rate I saw no more of them, and when these Good Samaritans came along I knew I was safe."

"The lungs of that blackamoor are worth more to thee than many guns," laughed Sam Kittredge. "'T is a pity thou couldst not bottle up a few of his screeches to take with thee when thou goest abroad. They are of a sort to make a wildcat sick with envy." The men laughed heartily, and, leaving the Goodman and Daniel with Sam, returned to their interrupted tasks.

Goodwife Kittredge insisted on their resting there for the night before resuming their journey. "You must be proper tired," said she, with motherly concern, "and if you go on now 't is more than likely those rascally knaves will follow you like your shadow. You'll stand a sight better chance of safety if you make an early start in the morning."

"Your horse needs rest, too," added Sam. "I'll rub her down and give her a measure of corn when she's cooled off. Get to bed with the chickens, and start with the sun, and to-morrow night will find you safe in your own home again."

To this plan the travelers gladly agreed. Early next morning, after a hearty breakfast in the Kittredges' cheerful kitchen they set forth once more. The roosters in the farmyard were still crowing, and the air was sweet with the music of robins, orioles, and blackbirds when they again plunged into the forest trail. All day they plodded steadily along, delayed by bad roads, and it was not until late that evening that they at last came in sight of the little house, where Nancy and her mother slept, little dreaming how near they were to a happy awakening. When at last they reached the cabin, the Goodman, fearing to alarm his wife, stopped on the door-stone and gently called her name. He had called but once when a shutter was thrown open and the Goodwife's head was thrust through it.

"Husband, son!" she cried joyfully. "Nancy!—awake child!—it is thy father and brother!" and in another moment the door flew open, and Nancy and her mother flung their arms about the necks of the wanderers. When the horse had been cared for, they went into the cabin. Nancy raked the coals from the ashes, the fire blazed up, and the Goodwife gave them each a drink of hot milk. Zeb blinked sleepily at the reunited and happy family, as Dan and his father told their adventures, and when at last they had gone to their beds in the loft he sank down on a husk mattress which the Goodwife had spread for him on the floor, and in two minutes was sound asleep.

V
THE NEW HOME

V

THE NEW HOME

GOODMAN PEPPERELL and his wife rose early the next morning, and, leaving the two children still sleeping, crept down the ladder to the floor below. There lay Zeb, also sound asleep, with his toes toward the ashes like a little black Cinderella. The Goodwife's mother heart was stirred with pity as she looked down at him. Perhaps she imagined her own boy a captive in a strange land, unable to speak the language, with no future but slavery and no friends to comfort his loneliness.

"Poor lad—let him sleep a bit, too," she said to her husband.

They unbolted the door and stepped out into the sunlight of a perfect June morning. The dew was still on the grass; robins and bobolinks were singing merrily in the young

113

apple trees, which, owing to a late, cold spring, were still in bloom, and the air hummed with the music of bees' wings.

The Goodman drew a deep breath as he gazed at the beauty about him. "'T is good to be at home again," he said to his wife. "And 't is a goodly land — aye, better even than old England! There's space here, room enough to grow." He looked across the river to the hills of Boston town. "I doubt not we shall live to see a city in place of yon village," he said; "more ships seek its port daily, and there are settlements along the whole length of the bay. 'T is a marvel where the people come from. The Plymouth folk are scattering to the north and south, and already villages are springing up between Plymouth and New Amsterdam. God hath prospered us, wife."

"Praise be to his holy name," said the Goodwife, reverently. "But, husband," she added, "what shall we do with our increase? Thou hast brought home a horse and the black lad. The horse can stay out of doors during the summer, but there is not room for him in the cow-shed, and the lad cannot sleep always before the fire."

"I have thought of that," said the Goodman, "and when the crops are in I purpose to build a larger house."

"Verily it will be needed," she answered. "The crops grow like weeds in this new soil. If there were but a place for storage, I could put away much for winter use that now is wasted. Go thou and look at the garden, while I uncover the coals and set the kettle to boil."

"Wait a moment, wife," said the Goodman, "I have somewhat to tell thee. There is ever a black spot in our sunshine. Though the danger grows less all the while as the settlements increase, it is still true that the Indians are ever a menace, and I fear they are over watchful of us." Then he told her of the attack in the forest. "I have reason to think the red-skins spied upon us all the way to Boston town," he finished. "I did not tell Daniel, but twice I saw savages on our trail after we left Kittredge's. I wounded one in the encounter, and they will not forget that. I know not why they should plot against the black boy, unless it is to revenge themselves upon me, but it is certain they tried to drag him away with them into the woods." The Goodwife listened with a pale face.

"'T is well, then, that we have a watchdog added to our possessions," she said at last. "Gran'ther Wattles's shepherd hath a litter of pups, and he hath promised one to the children. Nancy hath waited until Dan came home that he might share the pleasure of getting it with her."

"She hath a generous heart," said her father, tenderly. "Aye, — she is a good lass, though headstrong."

When their mother reached the cabin, she found the Twins up and dressed and Daniel trying to rouse the sleeping Zeb. "Wake up," he shouted, giving him a shake. Zeb rolled over with a grunt and opened his eyes.

"Take him outdoors while I get breakfast," said the Goodwife. "Mercy upon me, what shall I do with a blackamoor and a dog both underfoot!"

"A dog!" cried Daniel. "What dog? Where is he?"

"Nancy will tell thee," said his mother, and, not able to wait a moment to hear and tell such wonderful news, the two children rushed out at once, followed by Zeb. When their mother called the family to breakfast half an hour later, Zeb had been shown the garden, the corn-field, the cow-shed, the pig-sty, the straw-stack where eggs were to be found, the well with its long well-sweep, and the samp-mill. He had had the sheep pointed out to him, and been introduced to Eliza, the cow, and allowed to give Penny a measure of corn. The children had shouted the name of each object to him as they had pointed it out, and Zeb had shown his white teeth and grinned and nodded a great many times, as if he understood.

"I know he's seen eggs before, for he

117

sucked one," Dan told his mother. Zeb was
given his breakfast on the door-stone, and
Dan tried to teach him the use of a spoon,
without much success; and afterwards he
was brought in to family prayers. His eyes
rolled apprehensively as he looked from one
kneeling figure to another, but, obeying
Dan's gesture, he knelt beside him, and for
ten minutes he stuck it out: then, as the
prayer continued to pour in an uninterrupted
stream from the Goodman's lips, he quietly

crawled out on all fours and disappeared through the door. Dan found him afterwards out by the straw-stack, and as there was a yellow streak on his black face, concluded he had learned his lesson about the hen's nest altogether too well. He was given a hoe and taken to the corn-field at once. Here Daniel showed him just how to cut out the weeds with the hoe and loosen the earth about the roots of the corn. Zeb nodded and grinned so cheerfully that, after watching him a few moments, Daniel called Nancy and they started for Gran'ther Wattles's house in the village to get the puppy. They had gone but a short distance when Nancy, glancing around, saw Zeb following them, grinning from ear to ear.

" No — no — no — go back," bawled Daniel, pointing to the corn-field. Zeb nodded with the utmost intelligence and followed right along. "Oh, dear!" groaned Daniel. "I 've taught him to do things by showing how, and now he thinks he must do *everything* that I do."

He sat down on a stone and gazed despairingly at Zeb. Zeb promptly sat down on another stone and beamed at him! In vain Daniel pointed and shouted, and shook his head. Zeb nodded as cheerfully as ever and conscientiously imitated Dan's every move. In spite of all they could do he followed them clear to Gran'ther Wattles's house.

"Oh, dear!" said Nancy, "it's just like having your shadow come to life! You'll have to work all the time, Dan, or Zeb won't work at all!"

Even with the wonderful new puppy in his arms Dan took a gloomy view of the situation. "I'm sick of being an example," he said. "I had to be one at Aunt Bradford's all the time, for she told Mercy and Joseph to watch how I behaved, and now here's this crazy blackamoor mocking everything I do! I guess Father'll wish he had n't bought him."

The days that followed were trying ones for everybody. The Goodwife was nearly distracted trying to house her family and do her work in such crowded quarters. Zeb followed Dan like a nightmare, and the Goodman delved early and late to catch up with the work which had waited for his return. Among other duties there were berries to be picked in the pasture and dried for winter use, and this task fell to the children. It was work which Zeb thoroughly enjoyed, but alas, he ate more than he brought home. On one occasion he ate green fruit along with the ripe, and spent a noisy night afterward holding on to his stomach and howling at each new pain. In vain the Goodwife tried to cure him with a dose of hot pepper tea. Zeb took just enough to burn his mouth and, finding the cure worse than the disease, roared more industriously than ever. She was at her wit's end and finally had to leave him to groan it out alone beside the fire. It was weeks before he learned to understand the simplest sentences, and meanwhile poor Dan had to go on being an example.

Finally one day the Goodman brought home a large saw from Boston, and he and Dan showed Zeb how to use it. Then day after day Dan and Zeb sawed together, making boards for the new house, while Nancy brought her carding or knitting and sat on a stump near by with the puppy at her feet or nosing about in the bushes. They had named the dog Nimrod, " be-

cause," as Nancy said, "he is surely a
mighty hunter before the Lord, just like
Nimrod in the Bible. He sniffs around after
field mice all the time, and if he only sees
a cat he barks his head off and tears after
her like lightning!"

The summer passed quickly away, with
few events to take them outside the little

123

kingdom of home in which they lived. Twice
the Captain stopped to see them when the
Lucy Ann put in at Boston Harbor, and it
was from him they got such news as they
had of the world without. By October,
Nimrod had grown to be quite a large dog
and was already useful with the sheep, and
Zeb could understand a good deal of what
was said to him, though it was noticeable
that he was very dull when it concerned
tasks he did not like. With Dan to guide
him he was able to help shock the corn and
pile the pumpkins in golden heaps between
the rows. He could feed the cattle and milk
the cow and draw water for them from the
well. While the Goodman and the two boys
worked in the fields gathering the crops,
Nancy and her mother dried everything
that could be dried and preserved everything that could be preserved, until there
was a wonderful store of good things for
the winter.

One day when all the rafters were
festooned with strings of crook-necked

squashes, onions, and seed corn braided in long ropes by the husks, the Goodman appeared in the doorway with another load of seed corn and looked in vain for a place to put it.

"There is no place," said the Goodwife. "The Lord hath blessed us so abundantly there is not room to receive it. As it is, I can hardly do my work without stepping on something. If it is not anything else, it is sure to be either Zeb or Nimrod. Truly I can no longer clean and sand my floor properly for the things that are standing about."

The Goodman sat down on the settle and looked long and earnestly at the crowded room, whistling softly to himself. Then he rose and went to the village, and as a result the neighbors gathered the very next week to help build the new house. They came early in the morning, the men with axes and saws on their shoulders and the women carrying cooking-utensils. Then while the men worked in the forest felling trees, cutting and hauling timbers, and putting them in place, the women helped the Goodwife make whole battalions of brown loaves and regiments of pies, beside any number of other good things to eat. Nancy, Dan, and Zeb ran errands and caught fish and dug clams and gathered nuts to supply materials for them, and were promptly on hand when meal time came.

There were so many helpers that in a wonderfully short time the frame-work was up, the roof boards were on, and a great fireplace had been built into the chimney in the new part of the house. Also a door had been cut through to connect the new part with the old cabin, which was now to be used for storage and as a stable for Penny and Eliza, and a sleeping-space for Zeb. When all this was done and the roof on, the neighbors returned to their own tasks, leaving the Pepperells to lay the floors, cover the outside with boards, and do whatever was necessary to finish the house. It was late in the fall before this was accomplished and the family had settled down to the enjoyment of their new quarters.

One day as Dan and Zeb were bringing in boards to sheathe the room on the inside, they were startled to see two Indians peering out at them from the shelter of the near-by woods. Dropping the board they were carrying, they ran like deer to the house, and Dan told his father what they had seen. The Goodman looked thoughtful as he went on with his task of sheathing, and that very evening he worked late building a secret closet between the chimney and the wall. "It will be a handy place to hide thy preserves," he said to his wife, "and a refuge should the Indians decide to give us trouble." He cut a small square window high up in the outside wall and contrived a spring, hidden in the chimney, to open the door. When this spring was pressed a hole would suddenly appear in what seemed a solid wall, revealing the well-stored shelves. This closet was the Goodwife's special pride, but to Zeb it was a continuous mystery. At one moment there was the solid wall; the next, without touch of human hands, a door would fly open, giving a tantalizing glimpse of things to eat which he could never touch, for if he came near, the door would close again as mysteriously as it had opened. Dan loved to tease him with it, and Zeb, fearing magic, would take to his heels whenever this marvel occurred.

One day the Goodman said to his wife: "Thanksgiving draws near, and surely we have much cause for thankfulness this year, for the Lord hath exceedingly blessed us. There are yet some things to be done before the day comes, and I wish to meet it with my task finished. I hear there is a ship in the harbor loaded with English merchandise, and to-morrow I go to Boston, and if thou art so minded, thou canst go with me."

This put the Goodwife in quite a flutter of excitement, for she had not been away from home except to go to church for many months. She got out her best gown that very evening, to be sure it was in proper order, and while she got supper gave Nancy and Dan an endless string of directions about their tasks in her absence.

Early the next morning she mounted the pillion behind her husband, and the three children watched their departure, Dan clutching Nimrod, who was determined to go with them, and the Goodwife calling back last instructions to the little group until Penny was well on the road to Charlestown.

The house seemed strangely lonely without the mother in it, but there was no time for the children to mope, for there was all the work to do in their parents' absence. Dan took command at once. "You'll both have to mind me now," he said to Nancy and Zeb. "I'm the man of the house."

"If thou'rt the man of it, I'm the woman, and thou and Zeb will both have to do as *I* say," retorted Nancy, "or else mayhap I'll get thee no dinner! Mother said I could

make succotash, and thou lov'st that better
than anything. Mother said above all things
not to let the fire go out, for it would be
hard to bring a fire-brand all the way from
the village. So do thou bring in a pile of
wood and set Zeb to chopping more."

Dan counted his chances. "Very well," he said at last, with condescension, "thou art a willful baggage but I 'll give thee thy way! Only make the big kettle full."

All that day Nancy bustled importantly about the house, with her sleeves rolled up and her skirts looped back under her apron in imitation of her mother. She was better than her word and made johnny-cake besides the succotash for dinner, and after they had eaten it said to Dan, "If thou wilt go out to the field and bring in a pump-kin, I 'll make thee some pies for supper."

Dan dearly loved pumpkin pie, and in his zeal to carry out the plan brought in two great yellow globes from the corn-field instead of the one Nancy had asked for. "Mercy upon us," said Nancy when he appeared, beaming, with one under each arm, "those would make pies enough for all Cambridge. Thine eyes hold more than thy stomach."

"There 's no such thing as too many pies," said Daniel stoutly, "and if there 's any pumpkin left over, I'll feed it to the pig."

"I'll tell thee what we will do," said Nancy. "We will make a great surprise for Mother and Father. When they come home they will be tired and hungry and ready for a grand supper. Do thou and Zeb run down to the bay and bring back a mess of clams. We'll have the table all spread and a bright fire burning to welcome them!"

Dan agreed to this plan and went out at once to call Zeb. He found him by the straw-stack with an egg in each hand. "Take them in to Nancy," commanded Dan, pointing sternly toward the house. Zeb had meant to dispose of them otherwise, for he had a bottomless appetite for eggs, but he trotted obediently to the house at Dan's order, and then the two boys started together for the bay, with Nimrod barking joyfully and running about them in circles all the way.

The fall days were short, and it was dusk before the evening chores were done, and

Dan came in to the bright kitchen with Zeb
and Nimrod both at his heels, and announced
that he had a hole in his stomach as big as
a bushel basket. For answer Nancy pointed
to four golden-brown pies cooling on a shelf,
and Dan smacked his lips in anticipation.
Zeb came alongside and, copying Dan,
smacked his lips too.

134

"Go away, both of you," said Nancy. "You can only look at them now, for I have everything ready for Father and Mother, and we must n't eat until they come."

Dan looked about the room to see what Nancy's surprise might be. It was a cheerful picture that met his eye. First of all there was Nancy herself with her neat cap and white apron, putting the finishing touches to the little feast she had prepared. She had spread the table with the best linen and decorated it with a bunch of red berries. She had even brought out the silver tankard from its hiding-place under the eaves of the loft and placed it beside her father's trencher. The clams were simmering on the fire, sending out an appetizing smell, and the brown loaf was cut. The hickory logs snapped and sputtered, and the flames danced gayly in the fireplace, setting other little flames dancing in the shining pewter dishes arranged on a dresser across the room. Nimrod was lying before the fire with his head on his paws, asleep, and Zeb,

135

squatted down beside him, was rolling his eyes hungrily in the direction of the pies.

"I hope they'll come soon," said Daniel, lifting the cover of the kettle and sniffing. "If they do not 't is likely they'll find me as dead as a salt herring when they get here."

Nancy laughed and, breaking a slice of brown-bread in two, gave a piece to each boy. "Take that to stay your stomachs," she said, "and, for the rest, have patience."

For a long time they waited, and still there was no sound of hoofs upon the road. Dusk deepened into darkness, and the harvest moon came out from behind a cloud and shed a silvery light over the landscape. Nancy went to the door and gazed toward the road.

"Dost think, brother, the Indians have waylaid them?" she asked Dan at last.

"Nay," answered Dan. "They are likely delayed at the ferry. Should the ferry-man be at his supper wild horses could not drag him from it, I'll be bound. They'll come

presently, never fear, but it will doubtless
grieve them much to see me lying stiff and
cold on the hearth! Nancy, thou takest
a fearful chance in denying thy brother
food."

But Nancy only laughed at his woe-
begone face. "Thou art indeed a valiant
trencher-man," she said. Then, suddenly
inspired, she brought him the extra pumpkin, which she had not used for the pies,
set it before him upon the hearth-stone,
and gave him a knife. "Carve thyself a jack-
o'-lantern," she said. "'T will take up thy
mind and make thee forget thy stomach."

Dan took the knife, cut a cap from the top of the pumpkin, and scooped out the seeds. Then he cut holes for the eyes and nose, and a fearful gash, bordered with pointed teeth, for the mouth, and Nancy brought him the stub of a bayberry candle to put inside. Zeb watched the process with eyes growing wider and wider as the thing became more and more like some frightful creature of his pagan imagination. They were just about to light the candle when Nimrod gave a sharp bark; there was a creaking noise outside, and Nancy, springing joyfully to her feet, shouted, "They've come!—they've come!" She was half-way to the door, when suddenly she stopped, stiff with fright.

There, looking in through the open shutter, was the face of an Indian! Dan and Zeb saw it at the same moment, and Nimrod, barking madly, rushed forward and leaped at the window. Giving one of his wildcat shrieks, Zeb instantly went up the ladder to the loft with the agility of a monkey. The head had bobbed out of sight so quickly that for an instant Nancy hardly believed her own eyes, but in that instant Dan had been quick to act. He pressed the catch concealed in the fireplace, and, springing to his feet, seized Nancy and dragged her back into the secret closet. They nearly fell over the pumpkin, which lay directly in their path, and it rolled before them into the closet.

Once inside, they instantly closed the door, and, with wildly beating hearts, sank down in the darkness. About a foot above the floor there was a small knot-hole in the door, which the Goodman had purposely left for a peep-hole, and to this Dan now glued his eyes. In spite of Nimrod's frantic barking the house door was quietly opened, and when the dog flew at the intruder, he was stunned by a blow from the butt end of a musket, and his senseless body sent flying out of the door by a kick from a moccasined foot.

Then two Indians crept stealthily into

the room. They were surprised to find it empty. Where could the children have gone? They prowled cautiously about, looking under the table and behind everything that might afford a hiding-place, and, finding no trace of them, turned their attention in another direction. Dan was already near to bursting with rage and grief over Nimrod, and now he had the misery of seeing the larger of the two Indians take his father's musket from the deer-horn on the chimney-piece, while the other, who already had a gun, with grunts of satisfaction took the silver tankard from the table and hid it under his deer-skin jacket. At first they did not seem to notice the ladder to the loft. Soon, however, they paused beside it, and after they had exchanged a few grunts the larger Indian began to mount. It was plain they meant to make a thorough search for the children who had so miraculously disappeared.

Dan remembered what his father had said about the Pequots; Nancy, with sick fear in her heart for Zeb, was shivering in a heap on the floor, her hands over her eyes, though that was quite unnecessary, since the closet was pitch dark. Dan found her ear and whispered into it a brief report of what he had seen. They could now hear the stealthy tread of moccasined feet above them on the floor of the loft.

"While they're upstairs," whispered Dan, "I'm going to slip out and get Father's pistol. It's hanging behind a string of onions, and they haven't found it."

"Oh, no!" gasped Nancy. She clung to him, and in trying to get up he struck the pumpkin, which rolled away toward the outside wall of the closet. Just then there was a fearful outburst of noise overhead. There was the sound of something being dragged from under a bed across the floor, something which clawed and shrieked and fought like a wildcat. There were grunts and the thump of moccasined feet dancing about in a lively struggle.

"Now is my chance," said Dan to him-

141

self, and, opening the door cautiously, he made a dash for the pistol and snatched it from its hiding-place. As he was leaping back to the closet, he saw the bayberry candle lying on the hearth, and in that instant a wonderful idea flashed into his mind. He picked up the candle, lit it from the flames, and scurried back to his hiding-place just as the legs of an Indian appeared at the top of the ladder. He shut the door swiftly behind him, and, giving the candle to Nancy, told her to set it inside the pumpkin. Crawling to the other end of the closet, Nancy did as she was bid, while Dan, with his eye at the peep-hole, watched the two Indians drag poor Zeb between them down the ladder and out the door.

Eager to see where they went, Dan climbed up to the little window of the closet and peered out into the night. By the moonlight he could see the two men dragging Zeb in the direction of the straw-stack. They were having a hard time of it, for Zeb struggled fiercely, and they had their guns and the tankard to take care of as well, and in addition, to Dan's horror, one of them was waving a burning brand which he had snatched from the fire in passing! Dan trembled so with excitement that he nearly fell from his perch, but kept his wits about him. "Give me the pumpkin," he said to Nancy, and when she reached it up to him, he set the lurid, grinning face in the window. "Now the pistol," he said, and, sticking the muzzle through the opening beside the jack-o'-lantern, he fired it into the air.

The shot was answered by a chorus of yells from the three figures by the straw-stack. Scared out of their wits by the unexpected shot and by the frightful apparition which suddenly glared at them out of the darkness, the Indians took to their heels and ran as only Indians can run, dragging poor Zeb with them.

" They're gone," shouted Dan, dropping to the floor, "but they've set the straw-stack afire!"

By the dim light of the jack-o'-lantern

grinning in the window, he found the catch
of the door, and the two children burst out
of the closet. Seizing a bucket of water
which stood by the hand-basin in the corner, Dan dashed out of doors, followed by
Nancy, whose fear of Indians was now
overmastered by fear of fire. If their beautiful new house should be burned! She ran
to the well-sweep, and while Dan worked
like a demon, stamping on burning straws

with his feet, and pouring water on the
spreading flames, she swiftly plunged first
one bucket, then another, into the well and
filled Dan's pail as fast as it was emptied.
In spite of these heroic efforts the fire
spread. All they could do was to keep the
ground wet about the stack and watch the
flying sparks lest they set fire to the house.
Over the lurid scene the jack-o'-lantern
grinned down at them until the candle sputtered and went out.

The straw-stack was blazing fiercely,
lighting the sky with a red glare, when in
the distance they heard the beat of a drum.
Gran'ther Wattles had seen the flames and
was rousing the village. Then there were
hoof-beats on the road, and into the fire-
light dashed Penny with the terrified Goodman and his wife on her back. Once they
knew their children were safe, they did not
stop for questions, but at once set to work
to help them check the fire, which was now
spreading among the dry leaves. The Goodwife ran for her broom, which she dipped

in water and then beat upon the little flames
as they appeared here and there in the
grass. The Goodman mounted to the roof
at once, and, with Dan to fetch water and
Nancy to bring up buckets from the well,
they managed to keep it too wet for the

flying sparks to set it afire. At last the neighbors, roused by Gran'ther Wattles's frantic alarm, came hurrying across the pastures; but the distance was so great that the flames had died down and the danger was nearly over before they arrived.

There was now time for explanations, and, surrounded by an eager and grim-visaged circle, Nancy and Dan told their story.

"There's a brave lad for you!" cried Stephen Day, when the tale was finished, patting Dan on the shoulder. "Aye, and a brave lass, too," added another. Their father and mother said no words of praise, but there was a glow of pride in their faces as they looked at their children and silently thanked God for their safety.

"We can do nothing to-night," said Goodman Pepperell at last, "but, neighbors, if you are with me, to-morrow we will go into the woods and see if we can find any trace of the black boy. Doubtless by stealing him and burning the house they thought to revenge themselves for the Indian whom I wounded on my way home from Plymouth. They must have been watching the house, and, seeing us depart this morning, knew well that they had naught but children to deal with."

"Aye, but such children!" said Stephen Day, who had been greatly impressed by the story of the jack-o'-lantern. "We'll follow them, indeed, and if we find them"

148

—his jaw shut with a snap and he said no more.

While the men laid their plans for the morrow, the children and their mother stole round to the front of the house, and Dan began a search for Nimrod. He had been neither seen nor heard since the Indian had given him that fearful blow and thrown him out. They found him lying a few feet from the

house still half stunned, and Dan lifted him
tenderly in his arms, brought him into the
house, and laid him down before the fire,
where he had slept so peacefully only one
short hour before. Nimrod licked his hand,
and rapped his tail feebly on the hearth-
stone. Nancy wept over him, while Dan
bathed his wounded head, and tried to find
out if any bones were broken.

"Poor Nimrod," said the Goodwife, as
she set a bowl of milk before the wounded
dog, "thou art a brave soldier. Drink this
and soon thou wilt be wagging thy tail as
briskly as ever."

She stirred the fire and lit the candles,
and when the Goodman came in a few moments later, the little family looked about
their new home to see what damage had
been done. Nancy's little feast was a sad
wreck. There were the pies, to be sure, but
the table-cloth was awry and the flowers
were tipped over and strewn about the
floor, which was covered with the tracks
of muddy feet. In the scuffle with Zeb the

spinning-wheel had been overturned and the settle was lying on its back on the floor. The room looked as if a hurricane had passed through it. The Goodman mourned the loss of his gun, and the Goodwife grieved for her tankard, but all smaller losses were forgotten in their distress about Zeb. Not only had he cost the Goodman a large sum of money, but in the weeks he had been with them he had found his own place in the household, where he would be sadly missed. Worst of all was their anxiety about his fate at the hands of the Indians.

"Come," said the Goodwife at last, when they had heard every event of the day twice over, "we must eat, or we shall have scant courage for the duties of the morrow. We have none of us tasted food since noon."

The clams were still simmering gently in the pot, and she gave them each a porringer of broth, which they ate sitting in a circle about the hearth-stone. Then she put the room in order, and though her heart was heavy, tried to talk of the events of

their day in Boston as if nothing had happened.

"We saw Captain Sanders in town," she
said to the children. " He hath brought the
Lucy Ann to port with a load of cod for

the market and with fish and game for
Thanksgiving. I have his promise that he
will dine with us if God wills. He hath not
yet seen our new house. Alas! I shall have
no tankard to set before him; yet, ungrate-
ful that I am, we are still rich in blessings!
'T is well we have a day set aside to remind
us of them."

It was very late when at last the excitement had died down enough to think of
sleep. The Goodman went out to make sure
there was no fire left lurking in the grass,
and to take a look at the horse and cow.
As. he passed the smoking ashes of the
straw-stack, his foot struck something which
rang like metal, and in the moonlight something glistened in the path before him.
Stooping, he felt for it, and was overjoyed
to grasp the tankard, which the Indian had
lost in the struggle with Zeb. He carried it
in to his wife at once. She seized it with a
cry of joy.

"'T is a good omen," she said. "Mayhap thou 'lt find thy musket too." Her hus-

band shook his head gravely. "I'll have need of one to-morrow," he said. "'T is well I still have my fowling-piece and my pistol." Then he called the family together and, kneeling beside the settle, committed them to God's keeping for the night.

VI
HARVEST HOME

VI
HARVEST HOME

BEFORE daylight the next morning the
Goodwife stood in the door of the new
house and watched her husband set forth
with the men of Cambridge to search the
forest for Zeb, and to punish his captors if
they should catch them. She had given him
a good breakfast and filled his pockets with
bread for the journey, and when the men
came from the village, she cut Nancy's pies
and gave them each a generous piece to
eat before starting. There were eight men
in the party, all armed. The Goodwife's lip
trembled a little and then moved in prayer
as she saw them disappear into the dark
forest. "God grant that they may all return in safety," she murmured, and then,
giving herself a little shake, she turned back

into the house and resolutely set herself at the duties of the day.

Nimrod whined and tried to follow his master as the men marched away with their guns on their shoulders, but, finding himself too weak, lay down again on the hearth and went to sleep. The Goodwife cleaned the kitchen, removing the last traces of the intruders, and then began a patient march back and forth, back and forth, beside the whirling spinning-wheel. Now that the harvest was over and their food provided for the winter, her busy hands must spin the yarn and weave the cloth to keep them warm. Though she had meant to let the children sleep after the excitement of the previous day, it was still early when they were awakened by the whir of the wheel and came scuttling down from the loft as bright-eyed as if the adventures of the night before had been no more than a bad dream. They helped themselves to hasty pudding and milk and took a dishful to Nimrod, who was now awake and looking much more lively, and then their mother set them their tasks for the day.

"Nancy," said she, "I gave all thy pies to the men who have gone with father to hunt for Zeb. To-morrow will be Thanksgiving Day and we shall need more. The mince pies are already prepared and put away on the shelves, and thou canst make apple and pumpkin both to set away beside them in the secret closet."

"That makes me think," said Daniel, and, touching the secret spring, he opened the door and rescued the jack-o'-lantern from the window-sill.

It was only a wilted and blackened old pumpkin that he brought to his mother, but she smiled at it and patted the hideous head. "He hath been a good friend to us, Dan," she said, "e'en as say the Scriptures, 'God hath chosen the weak things of the earth to confound the mighty.' David went out against Goliath with a sling and a stone, and thou hast overcome savages with naught but a foolish pumpkin."

Nancy took the grinning head and set it
on the chimney-piece. "Dear old Jacky,"
she said, "thou shalt come to our Thanksgiving feast. 'T is no more than thy due
since thou hast saved us from the savages."

"Nay, daughter," said her mother. "That
savoreth of idolatry. Give thy praise unto
God, who useth even things which are not

to bring to naught the things that are. 'T is but a pumpkin after all, and will make an excellent feast for the pig on the morrow. Daniel, go to the field and bring thy sister a fresh one for the pies and then hasten to thine own tasks. They wait for thee. While thy father is away searching for Zeb, thou must do his work as well as thine own."

"Dost think, Mother, that he will surely bring Zeb back in time for the feast?" asked Nancy anxiously.

"Let us pray, nothing doubting," answered the mother. "If it be God's will, they will return."

There was a tremor in her voice even as she spoke her brave words, for she knew well the perils of their search. All day long they worked, praying as they prepared the feast that they might share it a united family. Nancy made the pies, and Dan dressed a fowl, while their mother got ready a pot of beans, made brown-bread to bake in the oven with the pies, and steamed an Indian pudding. All day they watched the forest

for sign of the returning men. All day they listened for the sound of guns, but neither sight nor sound rewarded their vigilance.

Dusk came on. The Goodwife set a candle in the window, and when her other tasks were finished, went back to her spinning. Not a moment was she idle, nor did she appear to her children to be anxious, but as she walked back and forth beside her wheel Nancy heard her murmuring, "Because thou hast made the Lord, which is my refuge, even the most High, thy habitation, there shall no evil befall thee, neither shall any plague come nigh thy dwelling." Over and over she said it to herself, never slacking her work meanwhile.

The supper which Nancy prepared waited —one hour—two—after Dan had fed the cattle and brought in the milk, and still there was no sign of the searching party.

Suddenly Nimrod, from his place on the hearth, gave a short sharp bark, and, leaping to the window, stood with his paws on the sill, peering out into the darkness and whining. Dan was beside him in an instant. "I see them," he cried joyfully, "a whole parcel of them. They are just coming out from behind the cow-shed."

Nancy and her mother reached the window almost at the same moment, and as the shadowy figures emerged from behind the cow-shed the mother counted them breathlessly, "One—two—three—four—five—"

"There's Father!" shrieked Nancy.

163

"He's carrying something. Oh, dost think it is Zeb?"

"Six—seven—eight—*nine! ten!* There are ten men, when but eight set forth. Praise God, they have all come back!" cried the mother. Turning swiftly to the fireplace, she snatched from it a brand of burning pitch pine and, holding it high above her head for a beacon, ran out to meet them, with Dan, Nancy, and Nimrod all at her heels. The torch-light shone on stern and weary faces as the men drew near.

"All's well, wife," came the voice of the Goodman.

"Hast found the lad?" she called back to him.

"Nay—not yet," he answered, "but we think we have his captors. Hold thy torch nearer and have no fear. The savages cannot hurt thee. Nancy, Daniel, have you ever seen these faces before?"

As he spoke he thrust forward two Indians with their hands securely tied behind them.

"Oh," shuddered Nancy, "I saw them at the window," and Dan added, "Aye, 'twas this one that kicked Nimrod." Nimrod confirmed his statement by growling fiercely and snapping at the heels of the taller of the two Indians.

"Call off thy dog," said the Goodman sternly, and though Dan felt it would be no more than fair to allow Nimrod one good bite, considering all he had suffered, he obediently collared Nimrod and shut him inside the kitchen. The faces of the Indians were like stone masks as they stood helpless before their captors with the light of the flaming torch shining upon them.

"Go in with thy family, Neighbor Pepperell," said Stephen Day. "There are enough of us and to spare to guard the savages. Mayhap a night in the stocks will cool their hot blood and help them to remember what they have done with the slave lad. If not, the judge will mete out to them the punishment they deserve."

"Right willingly will I leave them in

your hands," answered the Goodman, " for truly I am spent."

Whether the Indians understood their words, or not, they knew well the meaning of pointed guns, for they marched off toward the village without even a grunt of protest when Stephen Day gave the word of command.

The Goodman was so weary that his wife and children forbore asking questions until he was a little rested and refreshed. He sank down upon the settle with Nimrod beside him, and Dan removed his muddy boots, and brought water for him to wash in, while Nancy and her mother hastened to put the long-delayed supper on the table.

"This puts new life into me," declared the father when he had eaten a few spoonfuls of hotchpot, "and now I'll tell somewhat of the day's work. There was no general uprising among the Indians. At least we saw no evidence of it. 'T is more likely as I feared — they are the same Indians that followed us from Plymouth, meaning to revenge themselves upon me for wounding one of them when they set upon us in the forest."

"But how is it the lad was not with them?" asked his wife.

"That is a question which as yet hath no answer," replied her husband. "It may be they have killed him and hidden the body."

At this fearful thought Nancy shuddered and covered her face with her hands.

"It may be," went on the Goodman, "that they passed him on to some one else to avoid suspicion. At any rate he was not with them, and we could find no trace. Though the savages undoubtedly know some English, they refuse to say a word, and so his fate remains a mystery."

"What further shall you do to find him?" asked the Goodwife.

"See if we cannot force the Indians to confess, for the first thing," answered her husband.

His wife sighed. "I fear no hope lieth in that direction," she said. "Their faces were like the granite of the hills."

"What of the gun, Father?" asked Daniel. "Didst thou find it?"

"Nay," answered his father. "They had it not, and that causes me to think they have passed it as well as the boy on to others of their tribe. There is naught to be done now but wait until after Thanksgiving Day."

"'T will be but a sad holiday," said the Goodwife. "Though he is but a blackamoor, the lad hath found a place in my heart, and I grieve that evil hath befallen him."

"When I saw thee come out from behind the cow-shed I thought thou hadst a burden," said Daniel. "I thought it was Zeb —wounded, or mayhap dead."

"Aye," answered the Goodman. "I did carry a burden and had like to forgot it. I dropped it by the door of the cow-shed. Go thou and bring it in."

Dan ran out at once and returned a moment later carrying a huge wild turkey by the legs. His mother rose and felt its breast-bone with her fingers.

"'T is fine and fat, and young withal," she answered. "'T will make a brave addition to our feast on the morrow, for, truth to tell, our preparations have been but half-hearted thus far. Our minds were taken up with thy danger and fear for the lad."

"Dwell rather on our deliverance," said her husband. "The Lord hath not brought us into this wilderness to perish. Let us not murmur, as did the Children of Israel. The Lord still guides us."

"Aye, and by a pillar of fire, too," said Nancy, remembering the straw-stack.

"And instead of manna he hath sent this turkey," added Dan.

Supper was now over, and after it was cleared away, and they had had prayers, the mother sent the rest of the family to bed, while she busied herself with final preparations for the next day. She plucked and stuffed the great turkey, first cutting off the long wing-feathers for hearth-brooms, and set it away on the shelf in the secret closet along with Nancy's array of pies. It was late when at last she lit her candle, covered the ashes, and climbed wearily to bed.

The wind changed in the night and when they looked out next morning the air was full of great white snow-flakes, and the blackened ruins of the straw-stack were neatly covered with a mantle of white.

The family was up betimes, and as they ate their good breakfast of sausages, johnny-cake, and maple syrup, they sent many a thought toward poor Zeb, wandering in the forest or perhaps lying dead in its depths.

It was a solemn little party that later left the cabin in the care of Nimrod and started across the glistening fields to attend the Thanksgiving service in the meeting-house. They were made more solemn still by the sight of the two Indians sitting with hands and feet firmly fixed in the stocks, apparently as indifferent to the falling snow as though

they were images of stone. The first snow-
fall, usually such a joy to Nancy and Daniel, now only seemed to make them more
miserable, and they were glad to see the
sun when they came out of the meeting-
house after the sermon and turned their
steps toward home. At least Zeb would not
perish of cold if it continued to shine. They
were just beginning to climb the home hill,
when they were surprised to see Nimrod
come bounding to meet them, barking a
welcome.

"How in the world did that dog get out?"
said the Goodwife wonderingly. "I shut
him in the kitchen the last thing before we
left the house."

Leaving their father and mother to follow
at a slower pace, Nancy and Dan tore up
the hill and threw open the kitchen door.
There, comfortably dozing on the settle by
the fire, sat the Captain! At his feet lay
Zeb — also sound asleep with the wreckage
of several blackened eggs strewn round him
on the hearth-stone! The Captain woke

with a start as the children burst into the room and for an instant stood staring in amazement and delight at the scene before them. Zeb, utterly worn out, slept on, and the Captain, as usual, was the first to find his tongue.

"Well, well," he shouted, rubbing his nose to a bright red to wake himself up, "here ye be! And mighty lucky, too, for I'm hungry enough to eat a bear alive. If I could have found out where ye hide your supplies, I might have busted 'em open to save myself and this poor lad from starvation. He appeared nigh as hungry as I be, but he knew better how to help himself. He found these eggs cooked out there in the ashes of the straw-stack, and all but et 'em shells and all. Never even offered me a bite! Don't ye ever feed him?"

Before the children could get in a word edgewise their father and mother, followed by Nimrod, came in, and, what with the dog barking, the children screaming explanations to the Captain, and their own

astonished exclamations, there was such a
babel of noise that at last Zeb woke up, too,
and stared about him like one dazed. Nimrod jumped on him and licked his face, and
Zeb put his arms around the dog as if glad
to find so cordial a welcome. The Captain
stared from one face to another, quite unable to make head or tail of the situation.

"Well, by jolly!" he shouted at last,
"what ails ye all? Ye act like a parcel of
lunatics!"

The Goodman commanded silence, and
briefly told the whole story to the Captain.

"Where did you find the lad?" he asked, when he had finished.

"He was here when I came," said the Captain. "Settin' on the hearth-stone eatin' them eggs as if he had n't seen food fer a se'nnight and never expected to see any again. The dog busted out of the house when I came in, and as I could n't get any word out of the lad, I just set down by the fire and took forty winks. It was too late for meeting, and besides I reckoned I could sleep better here." He finished with his jolly laugh.

Zeb, meanwhile, sat hugging the dog and rolling his eyes from one face to another as if in utter bewilderment. Perhaps he wondered if the Captain meant to capture him, too, for life must have seemed to the poor black boy just a series of efforts to escape being carried off to some place where he did not wish to go, by people whom he had never seen before. The Goodman at last sat down before Zeb on the settle and tried to get from him some account of what had happened in the forest. But Zeb was totally unable to tell his story. His few words of English were inadequate to the recital of the terrors of the past twenty-four hours.

"Let the lad be," said the Goodwife at last. "He's safe, praise God, and we shall just have to wait to find out how he managed to escape from the savages and make his way back here." She went to the secret closet and brought out a huge piece of pumpkin pie. Zeb's eyes gleamed as he seized it. "He mustn't eat too much at once," said she. "As nearly as I can make out by the shells, he's had six eggs already. That will do for a time. Dan, build a fire in the fireplace in the old kitchen. There's warm water in the kettle, and do thou see that Zeb takes a bath. He is crusted with mud. He must have wallowed in it. Nancy and I will get dinner the while."

Dan beckoned to Zeb, and the two boys disappeared. Zeb had never bathed before except in the ocean, and the new process did not please him. "I believe he wished he'd stayed with the Indians," said Dan when he appeared an hour later followed by a well-polished but somewhat embittered Zeb. "I've just about taken his skin off and I'm all worn out. Oh, Mother, isn't dinner almost ready?"

"Almost," said his mother, as she opened the oven door to take a peep at the turkey, which had been cooking since early morning. "It only needs browning before the fire while I make the gravy."

The table was already spread, and Nancy was at that very moment giving an extra polish to the tankard before placing it beside the Captain's trencher. The spiced drink to fill it was already mulling beside the fire with a huge kettle of vegetables steaming beside it. The closet door was open, giving a tantalizing glimpse of glories to come.

"So there's where ye keep 'em," observed the Captain, regarding the pies with open admiration. "'T is a sight to make a man thankful for the room in his hold. By jolly, it'll take careful loading to stow this dinner away proper!"

He called Nancy to his side and opened the bulging leather pocket which hung from his belt. "Feel in there," he said. "I brought along something to fill in the chinks."

Nancy thrust in her hand, and brought it out filled with raisins. "I got 'em off a ship just in from the Indies," explained the Captain. Raisins were a great luxury in the wilderness, and the delighted Nancy hastened to find a dish and to place them beside the pies.

"All ready," said the mother at last. "Come to dinner."

There was no need of a second invitation, and the response to the summons looked like a stampede. The Goodman and his wife took their places at the head of the table with the Captain on one side and the children on the other, and because it was Thanksgiving, and because he had had such a hard day and night, and most of all because he was so clean, Zeb was allowed a place at the foot of the board.

The Goodman asked a blessing and then heaped the trenchers high with what he called the bounty of the Lord. There was only one cloud on Dan's sunshine during the meal. On account of Zeb, who when in doubt still faithfully imitated him, he was obliged to be an example all through the dinner. Even with such a model to copy, Zeb had great trouble with his spoon and showed a regrettable tendency to feed himself with both hands at once.

The turkey was a wonder of tenderness, the vegetables done to a turn, the Indian pudding much better than its name, and as for the pies, the Captain declared they were "fit to be et by the angels and most too good for a sinner like him."

Beside each plate the Goodwife had placed a few kernels of corn, and at the end of the feast, when the Goodman rose to return thanks, he took them in his hand.

"In the midst of plenty," he said to his

178

children, "let us not forget the struggles of the past and what we owe to the pioneers who first adventured into this wilderness and made a path for those of us who have followed them. Though they nearly perished of hunger and cold in the beginning, they failed not in faith. When they had but a few kernels of corn to eat, they still gave thanks, choosing like Daniel to live on pulse with a good conscience rather than to eat from a king's table. As the Lord prospered Daniel, so hath he prospered us."

Then they all stood with folded hands and bent heads, while he gave thanks for the abundant harvest and prayed that they might be guided to use every blessing to the honor and glory of God. And the Captain said, "Amen."

𝕿𝖍𝖊 𝕽𝖎𝖛𝖊𝖗𝖘𝖎𝖉𝖊 𝕻𝖗𝖊𝖘𝖘
CAMBRIDGE . MASSACHUSETTS
U . S . A